TOM SWIFT AND HIS FLYING LAB

The New Tom Swift Jr. Adventures
By Victor Appleton II

An object hurtling from the sky just missed them

THE NEW TOM SWIFT JR. ADVENTURES

TOM SWIFT
AND HIS FLYING LAB

by

VICTOR APPLETON II

Illustrated by Graham Kaye

SAMPSON LOW

LONDON

CONTENTS

ILLUSTRATIONS

Chapter I

A MESSAGE FROM SPACE

"HOW SOON will the Flying Lab be ready for the test hop, Tom?"

"In about two weeks, Dad. I can hardly wait to take her up."

Mr. Swift looked admiringly at the eighteen-year-old inventor. Tom Jr. resembled his father and had the same deep-set eyes, but he was slightly taller and more slender. The youth and his distinguished parent, both widely known for their scientific achievements, were headed for their experimental station, Swift Enterprises. There the Flying Lab had been built in a mammoth underground hangar.

"The atomic-powered engines should give us a speed of better than a thousand miles an hour, and the jet lifters——"

Tom was cut short by an uncanny whistling roar. An object hurtling from the sky just missed them, its turbulent backwash sprawling them on the ground, as it disappeared over the wall of Swift Enterprises. A split second later there was a tremendous thud and the earth shook.

"A bomb!" Tom shouted, jumping up.

"Or a meteor!" his father exclaimed.

By now both were running at top speed toward the private entrance to Swift Enterprises. Tom whipped an electronic key from his pocket and beamed it on the hidden mechanism. The gate flew open.

Inside the grounds there was pandemonium. Workers were racing from the cluster of buildings toward a gaping hole at the end of the airfield. Tom quickly out-distanced his father and was one of the first to reach the spot. In the earth yawned an immense crater.

"Gosh!" cried a workman. "You could fit a fire-house into that hole!"

The object that had bolted from the sky was buried too deeply to be seen, and the dirt at the edges of the pit had begun to cave in.

"What is it?" asked Hank Sterling, the chief engineer of the pattern-making division.

Tom shook his head. "I guess we'll have to dig around it to find out. Was anybody hurt?"

"I believe not."

Fortunately no one had been near the immediate area. Glass in several of the buildings had been broken, however, and various small articles jolted from shelves and desks.

By this time Mr. Swift had come up, and he immediately ordered a crew to start digging. Tom and Hank were so eager to learn what the object was that they brought out the big hydraulic shovel.

An hour later all the earth had been cleared from around the missile, and a ladder was lowered into the pit. Tom hastened down.

"It's not a natural meteor," he decided, as he examined the strange carvings on the side of the black cigar-shaped device. "It is mechanically made and only beings of high intelligence could have worked out those mathematical symbols."

Mr. Swift and Hank climbed down the ladder. They, too, were fascinated by the markings on the projectile.

"Do you think this was rocketed into space by creatures on another planet," Hank asked, "and that they were trying to send a message to Earth? It might even have been meant for you Swifts."

"If so, the meteor was launched with pin-point precision," Tom remarked.

"Have you any idea what those symbols mean?" Hank asked.

"I believe they're a code expressed in equations," Mr. Swift answered.

He and Tom pulled notebooks from their pockets and began to do some figuring. After covering a page, Tom looked up, a baffled expression on his face.

"It will take more than one notebook to work this out," he said. "It will have to wait. I want to find out if the earth tremor damaged the Flying Lab."

He hurried up the ladder, followed by his father and Hank. The Swifts retraced their steps to a building near the private entrance. Its roof was large and flat and only a few feet above the ground. Once more Tom took the electronic key from his pocket and flicked it to another combination.

The door to the underground hangar opened. He and his father descended the long, wide stairway of burnished steel.

Before them on the underground floor stood the Flying Lab, its tremendous silver body and V-swept wings almost filling the hangar. At first glance, no damage was apparent, but Tom went methodically from section to section before he was satisfied that no harm had come to his prized ship.

Meanwhile, Mr. Swift had gone to the private office in the underground hangar, which he shared with Tom, to continue working on the mathematical puzzle which had come hurtling out of space. In this office the Swifts' most valuable plans were kept and secret conferences were held. Tom arrived presently to report that the Flying Lab had not been damaged.

"If she weathered that earth tremor," Mr. Swift remarked, "she certainly is a sturdy bird. You can be proud of her, Tom."

"But even with the atomic engines and jet lifters, she'd never be able to stay in flight without your wonderful invention, Dad—the one Mother named after us."

"Oh, you mean the Tomasite plastic," Mr. Swift said. "Anyway, encasing the nuclear reactors with it is better than the old-type lead and concrete shields, and I believe it will absorb the radiation more effectively."

Mr. Swift took great delight in the fact that Tom, from earliest childhood, had shown all his father's flair for invention. As soon as the boy was old enough to study science, his father had been his teacher. As a result, Tom was known as one of the best-informed young inventors in the entire country.

Furthermore, because of his great interest in flying, Tom had become an expert pilot and had learned everything there was to know about the building of aircraft. A few months before, he had surprised his father with the idea of a flying laboratory to use in experiments.

For several years Mr. Swift had been convinced that both the ionosphere and the earth's depths held valuable secrets which could be useful to man. When Tom had shown him plans for the Flying Lab, he had urged his son to build the mammoth ship without delay.

"Did you figure anything out of those symbols?" Tom asked his father.

"Not yet. This quadrant within a quadrant——"

Mr. Swift's voice faded as he started further calculations. As Tom took out a pencil to work on the equation the telephone rang.

"Tom Swift Jr. speaking," he said.

"This is the *Shopton Evening Bulletin*. We understand a meteor fell in your grounds. But your guards won't let our reporter in!"

Tom smiled. The men at the gate obeyed orders under any circumstances!

"Sorry, Mr——"

"Perkins. We must have a story."

"I'll give it to you," Tom said quietly. "A huge piece of mineral buried itself in our airfield. We haven't had time to analyse it yet. We'll let you know later. No one was hurt and damage was slight."

"Is that all? How about a picture?"

"We'll take one for you." After Tom had hung up he looked at his father, his eyes twinkling. "Shall we take the picture without the symbols showing?"

"Yes, Tom. I'd like to wait a little longer before making them public. I almost believe Hank was right about the projectile being sent to you and me to figure out."

"Okay, Dad, we'll wait."

"Say, Tom, isn't it about time you wrote to Rip Hulse about the trial flight of the Flying Lab?" Mr. Swift asked.

"I'll do it today."

Ripcord Hulse, an ace pilot, was a long-standing friend of the Swifts. He had seen the plans for the ship and had been promised a preview of her first flight.

Toward noon Tom was busy inspecting the landing

gear of the Flying Lab when a voice boomed through the hangar.

"Well, brand my fuselage! Looks like I jest got home in time! So this is what we're goin' to go gallivantin' 'round the world in, eh? Mighty fine, I'd say."

Sun-bronzed Chow Winkler, the rotund, happy-go-lucky cook and steward on all Swift expeditions, stood grinning from the foot of the steps. He wore a flashy red-and-green checkered shirt and held a sombrero in one hand.

Tom leaped forward to greet the newcomer.

"Chow! Welcome back. How was your trip?"

"Fine. Ole Texas looked jest as good as it did years ago before I joined up with you. Had a great time seein' all my cowpoke friends. An'," he added proudly, opening his jacket and fingering his shirt, "I picked up this lil number in Fort Worth."

Tom covered his eyes with his hands.

"Ow! Those colours really dazzle!" Then he added warmly, "It's great to see you, Chow. We've missed you."

Chow, whose real name was Charles, had been a chuck-wagon cook in the Southwest for many years. He had become acquainted with Tom and his father while they were working on atomic research near a ranch at which Chow was employed at the time. It had not been long before he and Tom had become fast friends, and when the Swift expedition returned North, Chow had attached himself to the party.

"Say, a feller at the gate put this lil ole good-luck charm on my arm—an electric whatchamacallit!"

"You mean one of our electronic amulets." Tom laughed. "Without that little bracelet, Chow, you'd have our radarscopes working overtime."

"How come?" Chow asked.

"It sounds complicated, but it's really simple," Tom explained. "The little bracelet traps radar impulses and keeps them off our scopes. There's a giant scope on top of the main building now for everyone to see, and a special one down here in the office for the underground hangar.

"So," Tom went on, as Chow looked perplexed, "anyone who doesn't wear an amulet causes a little dot of light to show up on one scope or the other. That's how we can tell if a spy has sneaked in."

"Well, your ole radar kin have the day off, far as I'm concerned." Chow chuckled. "Jest thought I'd come 'round an' find out how you-all are."

"Wait until you see what we've set up for you in the Flying Lab," Tom said. "By the way, we're calling it the *Sky Queen*. Our three-decker has everything, including——"

"Three-decker? You mean this here *Sky Queen* has three floors?" Chow leaned so far back to look up at the big ship that he almost fell over on his balding head.

"That's right," Tom answered. "Come on. I'll show you around."

He climbed a ladder through a hatch beneath the wings. Chow followed.

"This first level is partly for storage," Tom explained as they stood inside. "We'll keep spare equipment, experimental supplies, and luggage down here. But look back in this end. See those sliding doors to the outside? Behind the doors is our hangar. We're going to carry two baby aircraft—a small jet plane we call the *Kangaroo Kub* and a jet-lifted helicopter, the *Skeeter*."

Chow's eyes widened. Then he said, "Where's the galley? We got to eat!"

"We'll come to it."

Next, they went up a flight of narrow, steel-ribbed stairs and into the larger sector of the ship's interior. Forward was the control room containing the pilot's and co-pilot's seats. Every bit of wall space was covered with dials, switches, and gadgets. Chow rubbed his eyes.

"Say, you'll need a big crew to push an' pull all those buttons an' levers."

Tom smiled. "Chow, this is so simply arranged that the Sky Queen could almost fly itself. The only men who'll be on the ship are Dad, my friend Bud Barclay, and you and I."

The cook, utterly amazed, shook his head.

"Where's the laboratory itself?"

"Mid-fuselage. It's partitioned off from the rest of the ship and is a soundproof, air-conditioned room, or series of rooms. One's my physics lab, another's for chemistry. Then there's a place for experiments with animals——"

"Hold on!" Chow begged. "We goin' to carry a zoo along?"

Tom laughed. "Some day perhaps."

He slid back the door and switched on a light. The huge room was partitioned off into cubicles with walls shoulder high. Chow gazed in awe at the physics division with its six-foot electron microscope and X-ray, ultra-violet and infra-red absorption apparatus.

He shook his head. "Mighty fine," he said, "but it's beyond me. I'll stick to my galley. Where is it?"

Tom chuckled at the cook's impatience as he led the way to the third deck. Forward was a comfortable windowed lounge, complete with easy chairs and a small library of scientific books and magazines. Back of this were the sleeping quarters, and in the rear was the galley. Chow surveyed the layout of modern equipment in pleased astonishment.

"Well, brand my skillet!" he said. "Will I cook up some fancy dishes!"

He was about to inspect his new quarters when Mr. Swift called up anxiously from the first deck. "Tom! Tom! Come to my office! Quick!"

Tom raced down the stairways and ladder and across the concrete floor to the office where his father stood with a smashed cathode-ray tube in his hands.

"What's up, Dad?"

"Our radar equipment—it's been broken!" Mr. Swift exclaimed. "And look at the time chart. An intruder was registered at 3 : 19 A.M. !"

"Someone without an amulet broke in here?" Tom cried incredulously.

Mr. Swift's face was stern. "Yes. And according to the time chart on the radar, someone who was looking around for five minutes before he broke the radar apparatus. No telling how long he was here after that, nor what it was he wanted."

"He's not hiding aboard the Flying Lab," Tom remarked. "I've just been all over her. Say, it's funny no one reported a dot on the outdoor radarscope. Maybe the intruder's still around!"

As Mr. Swift picked up the telephone to alert their private police, Tom rushed from the office and up the steps to the ground level. Dashing outdoors, he looked around.

By this time a number of uniformed guards were running to pre-arranged posts to investigate. Others were speeding away in cars so that every bit of the four-mile-square enclosure would be covered.

Tom stopped one of the guards and asked whether anything had been picked up on the master scope. The man said nothing had, and hurried away.

"The grounds are well covered," Tom remarked to himself. "But the spare-parts warehouse—no one's looking there!"

Tom ran to the big storage shed and hurried inside. He was just in time to see a short young man with sleek black hair turn and plunge out of a rear door. The man disappeared near some empty packing cases.

Tom raced after him. He was searching among the big crates when he heard a noise behind him. Turning, he caught a glimpse of glittering dark eyes.

Then came a crashing blow on his head. Tom sank to the ground unconscious!

Chapter II

SNEAK ATTACK

AS THE GUARDS fanned out over the grounds, Tom's father hurried up the hangar steps, opened the door, and looked around. A plant policeman, running toward him, cried out excitedly:

"No one's been caught yet, Mr. Swift, and the men found the big radarscope disconnected."

"What!"

"They've reported it to the engineers."

"Good! Where's Tom?"

Mr. Swift questioned several guards. In the excitement of the search not one of them had noticed the young inventor. Fearful that Tom might have stumbled into trouble, he was about to start a search of his own when a familiar voice hailed him.

"Mr. Swift! What's all the excitement about? That hole in the airfield, guards running around like crazy——"

The speaker was rugged Bud Barclay, Tom's best friend and co-pilot, whose family lived in San Francisco. Bud had been out testing the midget helicopter which was to go aboard the Flying Lab.

Mr. Swift hurriedly explained the morning's excitement.

"I'll help you hunt," Bud offered.

The nearest building was the large spare-parts shed.

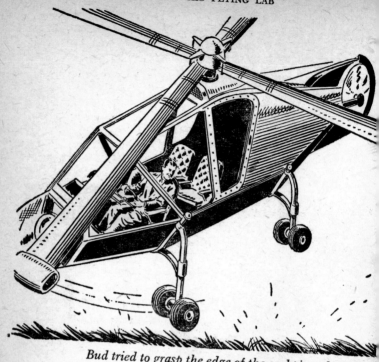

Bud tried to grasp the edge of the cockpit and

Dashing to the rear of it, he saw three guards combing the interior.

Outside were several empty packing cases. As Bud approached them, he tripped over a heavy tarpaulin bunched on the ground. Something beneath it moved! Tearing the canvas aside, Bud stared in shocked amazement.

Tom lay there unconscious!

Bud quickly examined his friend. Then he called a guard from inside the building to summon Mr. Swift.

"Tom's hurt!" he cried out.

pull himself up, but he missed by inches

Three minutes later the man returned, bringing the boy's father with him. Bud was already giving first aid. Mr. Swift asked the guard to fetch some cold water and a restorative. When these were brought, he administered them to the unconscious boy.

In a few moments Tom sat up and looked around dazedly.

"Are you all right?" his father and Bud asked anxiously.

"I think so. That guy really clipped me."

"What guy?" Bud demanded.

"The one I was chasing. I figured he was the fellow who'd been in our office."

"What did he look like?" Mr. Swift asked.

"Thin, dark, short. About twenty-five. Had black hair and dark eyes."

Mr. Swift immediately sent the guard to give Tom's description of the intruder to all employees at the plant.

Bud Barclay suddenly let out a cry. "Say, I left the *Skeeter* over in the woods beyond the runways. If that guy can fly, he may try to get away in it."

Almost before he finished speaking, Bud was sprinting toward the trees. An excellent football player and track man, he covered the distance in record time between the spare-parts shed and the woods at one end of the Swift Enterprises enclosure.

Just as Bud entered the woods, an engine whistled into life some distance ahead of him.

"If that's the same fellow who clipped Tom, I'm too late!" the co-pilot muttered.

Moments later he burst into the tiny clearing in which he had set the helicopter down. It was just taking off. Bud made a dash for the *Skeeter*, trying to grasp the edge of the cockpit and pull himself up before it rose out of reach, but he missed by inches. Nevertheless, he got a good look at the dark, sleek-haired pilot. Then the helicopter rose and swung out of sight over the trees.

"He can't get away with this!" Bud set his jaw. Dashing back to where Tom and his father were, he shouted, "He stole the *Skeeter*! But I'll take up a jet and try to force him down!"

"I'll go with you!" Tom exclaimed.

"Hold on!" Mr. Swift warned him.

"I'm all right, really I am, Dad!" Tom insisted.

"Are you certain, Tom? Better take it easy after that blow you got."

Tom nodded as he followed Bud to a hangar. A mechanic helped roll out one of the jets. Bud taxied into position and soon the plane was roaring into the air.

"The guy was headed this way," he said, making a turn south. "He hasn't had time to get very far."

But the boys discovered that their quarry must have moved a lot faster than they had thought possible. There was no sign of him as they flew back and forth over the countryside.

"But where'd he go?" Bud said, still dumbfounded over the stranger's speedy disappearance. "You can't set a helicopter down and hide it in such a short time."

"But *he* did," Tom replied, equally mystified.

Taking over the controls, he flew as close to the tree-tops as he dared, while Bud scanned the terrain. When they had failed to spot the helicopter, Tom climbed higher and Bud scrutinized the countryside through powerful binoculars. But the search proved fruitless, and the boys returned to Swift Enterprises' airfield.

Bud was very sober. "I'm responsible for the loss of the *Skeeter*," he said. "I should have locked it. But I'll get it back! Tom, that ship's a dream. She handles like a baby carriage. I can set her down on a dime and give you nine cents change."

"I hope it won't be long before you can do it again," Tom said. "I'll notify the police at once that the copter's gone."

After phoning the State Police, the boys went to the underground office and reported their failure to Mr. Swift. He was as puzzled as they over the helicopter's disappearance.

"It must have more forward speed than I suspected," he remarked.

"It has plenty," Bud remarked. "What I'd like to know is why that thief was snooping around here. Have you any idea, Mr. Swift?"

"I've been trying to find out," the scientist replied, "but there are so many drawings and pieces of equipment in these cabinets that would be useful to——"

During the conversation, Mr. Swift had been pulling out one drawer after another. Now he came upon one that was empty.

"I guess this is our answer," he said grimly. "The drawings and specifications for our super-Geiger counter are gone, Tom!"

"Wait a minute!"

The young inventor leaped across the room to another cabinet and yanked open the bottom drawer. A smile of relief spread over his face.

"Only half of the plans are gone, Dad. I put the others in here yesterday with the miniature model."

Bud burst into laughter. "What a surprise the Pomade Kid's going to get!" Then he became serious. "What I can't understand is how he got in here in the first place. He'd need a special key, wouldn't he?"

"You're right." Tom looked meaningfully at his father. "Do you think it might have been an inside job? Or a job with inside help?"

"That might account for the outdoor radar being tampered with," Bud suggested. "One of the plant workers might have disconnected it, then let his confederate in."

"I hate to be suspicious of anyone here," Mr. Swift remarked, "but I suppose we'd better consider every angle."

Hastening to the main office of the plant, where employees files were kept, he and the boys began a check-up. After a half-hour's inspection of records, they had found nothing questionable about any employee.

"We'll keep going," Mr. Swift said tensely, opening another drawer.

As they began scanning the second set of records, there was a knock on the door. Mr. Swift quickly put away the file while Tom went to see who the caller might be.

"Arthur Roberts is here," he announced over his shoulder.

Roberts had worked for many years at the Swift plant as a tool designer. The close, exacting skill had proved too great a strain on his eyes. As a result, he had been assigned the duty of chief night custodian at the experimental station.

"Tell him to come in," said Mr. Swift.

The moment the man appeared in the doorway, the three in the office knew something was wrong. Roberts' face was pale and drawn, and there were dark circles under his eyes. As he removed his cap slowly, they noted that his hand shook a little.

"Yes, Roberts," Mr. Swift said.

The man cleared his throat, then spoke gravely, "I have something to confess. I'm responsible for the theft of the super-Geiger counter plans."

Chapter III

A SCIENTIFIC THIEF

TOM and his father stared at the man in astonishment.

"You, Roberts?" Mr. Swift asked. "But you've been with us for years. You're one of our most trusted men."

Roberts looked down at the floor. "I know. But I couldn't help what happened."

"Tell us everything," Mr. Swift said.

"Last night," the guard began, "I had just unlocked the door to the underground hangar to make my hourly rounds when a strange man came up to me. He matches the description of the one who later knocked Tom out. I don't know how he got in—anyhow, it wasn't by the main gate. He said he was a member of Hemispak."

"Hemispak! The scientific society of the Americas!" Mr. Swift cried. "The group formed to pool information and resources for the protection of the Western Hemisphere!"

"I know how important Hemispak is, so I asked him what he wanted."

"And?"

"He said he wished to see your new Geiger counter plans."

"How did he know about that?" Tom exclaimed. "It's to be one of the secret gadgets of the Flying Lab!"

"I told him I couldn't allow that without permission from you, Mr. Swift," Roberts continued.

"Then what happened?"

"He pulled a gun. He said he'd been briefed on me —even knew about my son John being in South America. You know, John's a chemist there, and is doing work for Hemispak." Roberts lowered his voice. "Looking for uranium, I believe. That fellow said both John and his wife would be tortured if I didn't tell him where to find the plans."

"And you did?"

"I had no choice."

"So you took him to the underground office?" Tom asked.

Roberts nodded. "The man opened the file cabinets and started rummaging through them, still holding the gun on me. When he found the plans, I tried to grab them, but he hit me on the head with his gun and knocked me out. I was unconscious for hours—only woke up a little while ago in my own house."

"How'd you get there?" Bud asked.

Roberts shrugged wearily. "My wife said I came in at 4 A.M., but I don't remember a thing about it."

The others concluded that the guard had suffered a slight concussion and had gone home by himself without being aware of his actions.

"I hurried right over here to tell you what happened and to find out what else that thief took," Roberts said. "I feel very bad about last night."

"You're lucky to be alive," Tom remarked. "Well, to date, all we know is that our visitor has taken our small copter and half the plans for the super-Geiger counter."

"Half!" Roberts exclaimed. With a groan he added, "Then he'll be back for the rest."

"He won't dare!" Bud spoke up.

The night custodian was not so sure of this.

"There's something else I should tell you," he said. "I wrote to John about the super-Geiger counter. I hate to admit it—but my letter was probably opened by some enemy. Last night's theft was the result."

"I wonder," mused Mr. Swift, "if there might be a definite connection between your son's working for the Hemispak Scientific Society and our recent troubles here. I'd suggest that you cable John and warn him. If this *is* the work of some enemy group, they may carry out the threat against your family."

Roberts thanked his employer and hurried off to follow the elder Swift's advice. Left alone, the others discussed more effective security measures.

"How about setting up a television camera with recording film?" Tom suggested.

"Just the thing," his father agreed, and issued orders to the engineers to install several of these detectors, as well as repair both radar mechanisms.

"I'd certainly like to get my hands on that oily-haired sneak who conked you, Tom!" Bud burst out. The co-pilot's big shoulders strained at the seams of his heavy ribbed sweater. "I'd do a job on him!"

"I wouldn't mind getting a whack at him myself!" Tom retorted, his lean, strong hands clenching unconsciously.

"He sure knows how to handle a copter," Bud spoke up. "Maybe he landed inside our grounds in one of his own, back in the woods, and then had a confederate take it out while he went searching for the new Geiger counter plans."

"Could be," Tom said. "But I'll bet he came down a ladder from a copter. Then his buddy flew off and was coming back tonight to pick him up."

"But he got a free ride earlier," Bud said. "What I can't understand is why the master radarscope didn't detect him when he dropped in."

Tom snapped his fingers. "I have it! He has an amulet of his own or some other anti-radar device."

"Proving that he's a scientist, and a dangerous enemy," Mr. Swift said. "No doubt the pilot of the copter worked some device until his friend got down and disconnected our main radar set-up."

"But they couldn't know about the one in the underground hangar," Tom commented.

"Actually I don't feel too bad about the loss of those drawings," Mr. Swift said. "The invention hasn't come up to our expectations."

"What's wrong with it?" Bud asked.

"Not sensitive enough for long-range work. We had hoped to use it miles up in the air to detect minerals."

"On Mars?" Bud's imagination was stirred.

"It's possible." Mr. Swift smiled. "But actually we want to find out what unknown elements may be floating around in space.

"You see, when radiation from a disintegrating atom cuts through the gas in the tube, it sets off a tiny explosion. The gadget is hooked up to an amplifier, which magnifies this tiny explosion into a signal we can hear.

"The cosmic rays in the atmosphere make the counter click slowly, in what we call a 'background count.' But when the counter gets close to some uranium or radium, then it really begins to chatter.

"However, the signals we've been getting aren't strong enough to indicate that it will perform as we want it to from a distance."

"How about using a gas of heavier weight?" Tom suggested. "It might carry a stronger signal."

"You may have something there, son! A different mixture of gases might be just what we need."

Mr. Swift said he would go to the Flying Lab at once and start some experiments with gases of greater sensitivity. After he left the office, Bud said:

"Those million-dollar ideas are over my head. Listen, professor, how does a Geiger counter count, anyway? Does it say one, two, three, four?"

"Sure, sure," Tom replied, chuckling. "How did you ever pass your physics course?"

"Okay, the Geiger counter works on impulses," Bud said. "As I see it, inside the gas-filled tube is a colony of trained fleas. The near presence of uranium raises the temperature of the gas, giving the fleas the hot-foot."

"Right," Tom answered in mock seriousness. "Then the fleas do a tap dance which makes the clicking on the Gieger counter."

Bud burst into a laugh. "It serves me right," he said.

At this moment the inter-office phone rang. Tom picked it up.

"Your sister is at the main gate," Miss Trent, the Swifts' private secretary, informed him. "Sandy says something has happened. You're to come out there at once!"

Tom relayed the message to Bud, and the two boys hurried through the grounds, wondering what Sandra Swift was about to tell them. The attractive blonde girl, a year younger than her brother, resembled him in looks and disposition.

The boys found Sandy astride her horse, Jumper. His glossy coat was drenched with sweat from a hard run, and he was prancing about nervously. His owner, too, appeared to be excited.

"What's up?" Tom asked.

"Something awful happened a little while ago," Sandy burst out. "I was riding Jumper along Old Mill Pond Road when a tiny copter that looked just like your new one came down right in front of me!"

Tom and Bud looked at each other, speechless. The stolen aircraft!

"The pilot rolled it under some big willow trees," Sandy went on, "and then came tearing out into the middle of the road. He gave me a fearful scare. Ran right up to me and grabbed Jumper's bridle. But just then a farm truck came along. The pilot pulled out a gun and forced the driver to stop.

"He yelled to me not to dare tell anyone I'd seen him, and then climbed into the truck and made the driver start up again."

"He stole that copter from us!" Tom said, and quickly told Sandy the story of the theft. "We must get it back!"

"Do be careful," Sandy begged them. "That man has such a wicked face."

"Don't worry," Tom answered. "But there's no time to lose, Bud. Come on!"

Chapter IV

A CALL TO DANGER

FIFTEEN MINUTES later Tom and Bud pulled up in Bud's car at the place where the midget helicopter had been abandoned. It was well screened in a willow grove near a brook.

"No wonder we couldn't see it from the air," Bud grumbled as he opened the door. "The way those willow branches hang down, it might as well be draped with curtains."

The boys rolled out the *Skeeter* and Tom climbed in. A moment later he called down that apparently the thief had not meddled with the controls.

"I'll fly it back," he said. "See you at the plant."

With Bud driving far below, Tom gave the craft a good wringing out to be sure that the strange pilot had not tampered with any part of it. When Tom came down, he found Sandy waiting for him.

"I'm so glad you got the copter back," she said.

"So am I, Sandy. That squares up one of the thefts. But don't ride around alone on country roads any more."

"You bet I won't," she promised. "At least, not until they catch that horrible gunman!"

"I must call and tell the police we found the copter," Tom said.

He was informed by the police captain that he had

already heard the story from the truck driver and had sent out an alarm. Several days went by and still there was no trace of the thief.

Tom had plunged into his work on the Flying Lab, overseeing countless precision jobs on which the crew's lives would depend once they were airborne. This did not keep him from pulling out of his pocket many times a day a copy of the symbols on the strange missile that had fallen from the sky. Solving the mysterious message it seemed to convey had become a game between Tom and his father. At dinner each evening they would compare notes about the results of their calculations.

"Any progress, Tom?" Mr. Swift finally asked one night, a twinkle in his eyes.

Just that day Tom had computed the ratio of the diameters of a smaller to a larger circle and concluded that the large circle was meant to be Earth, the smaller one Mars. The message could be from Martian scientists.

"Yes, Dad, I have one theory," Tom replied. "Those two overlapping circles—they work out mathematically to represent this planet and Mars. Some people from up there must be trying to get an important message across to us."

Mr. Swift laughed. "Well, we're still running neck and neck in our race."

"I wish I had more time to work on the symbols," Tom replied. "But I'll certainly try to solve them before we take off for the ionosphere!"

Late one morning, after Tom had finished tabulating the contents of the storage compartment on the *Sky Queen*, he decided to go up to the galley. Seeing the workmen leave for lunch made him realize that he was hungry. On the way some open wiring caught his eye.

"Hm," Tom said to himself, studying it several seconds, "these wires run to the gyro-stabilizer. But they shouldn't cross the beam. At this stage they could cause a fire."

The young inventor pulled out his pocket flashlight and made a further examination. Though he felt he was right, Tom decided, before speaking to the workmen, to check the blueprint. He hurried down to the office and studied the detailed sheet a few moments. The wiring would have to be changed.

As Tom came from the office, he stopped short. Looking up, he was horrified to see wisps of smoke curling from the air vents of the Flying Lab! Visions of disaster flashed through his mind.

"But it's coming from the third deck," he observed. "It can't be that wiring."

Grabbing a fire extinguisher, Tom leaped up the interior stairway of the plane. He ran head on into a figure racing downward.

"Chow! What's on fire?"

The chef was coughing and choking as he tried to find his way down the steps, his eyes streaming with tears from the smoke.

"Lemme out."

"Is it in the galley?"

"Galley? No, no. The galley's not on fire. It's my invention burned up."

"Your invention?" Tom cried.

Chow held out his hand in which lay a black pellet. "This lil ole pill is all that's left," he said sadly. "Tom, this here is concentrated, dehydrated spinach—a kettleful."

Tom collapsed on the steps, roaring with laughter. "Sabotage of the Flying Lab—by spinach pills!" he howled.

Chow gave the inventor an indignant look, still coughing because of the smoke in his lungs.

"I'll make 'em work yet," he declared. "I was goin' to surprise you with spinach for lunch, but I'll fix somethin' else."

"A he-man steak, please," Tom begged.

When the electricians returned from lunch, Tom told them about the wiring, then he walked over to the office which he and Mr. Swift shared in the main building. His father was there and said:

"Roberts just had a cablegram from his son's wife. Young Roberts has gone into the mountains on an expedition with a group of scientists. I hope nothing happens to him."

Mr. Swift had barely conveyed this news when the intercom phone buzzed.

"There is someone at the gate to see you and your son," said Miss Trent.

"We're very busy," answered Tom's father. "You know when I'm——"

"I'm sorry, Mr. Swift. But I believe you'll want to see this man right away. He says he's from the Hemispak Scientific Society!"

Across the office, Tom and his father looked at each other in amazement.

From Hemispak! Could this be the same man who had attacked Roberts and Tom? Would he dare take a chance to come here again?

"Bring him in!" Mr. Swift told the secretary.

Before they arrived, Tom pushed a button and the

work-bench, covered with plans and gadgets, slid silently into the wall out of sight.

"We'd better watch him, Dad! Even if he isn't the same man, he may be a pal of his. I think we'd better keep him between us while he's in here."

"Good idea, Tom."

"Señor Carlos Ricardo," Miss Trent announced presently, and ushered the caller in.

Tom knew at once that he was not the man who had knocked him unconscious. The caller was older and less agile-looking.

"May I present my credentials, gentlemen?" the stranger said after the Swifts had introduced themselves. "I am the newly chosen president of the Hemispak Scientific Society."

He pulled a membership card and letters from a pocket to support his claim. The Swifts examined them and felt satisfied.

"We have heard a great deal about Swift Enterprises," Señor Ricardo began. "Hemispak hopes to have the pleasure of working side by side with the two famous Swifts."

"If Hemispak is all we've heard it is," Mr. Swift replied, "that would be a distinct privilege for us."

His suspicions, as well as Tom's had been completely dispelled by the stranger's straightforward manner.

"We have a great deal of work to do," went on Señor Ricardo, "but if we can maintain our ideals of co-operative scientific work in behalf of the northern and southern continents of America, the Western Hemisphere should benefit greatly."

The trio now relaxed in friendly, companionable conversation.

"Some day I'd like to visit South America again,"

Tom remarked. He did not say so, but in his mind he finished "—and in the *Sky Queen* would be the perfect way to do it."

"That may be sooner than you think," was the surprising answer. "Your own reputation, for one so young, is widely known among our people through the scientific journals. And that is part of my reason for coming to Swift Enterprises today."

Tom sat up expectantly.

"If I may acquaint you with certain facts," Señor Ricardo remarked, "my country is having trouble with a certain group of its people—the Veranos. Verano is really a splinter state, run by rebels who broke away from the mother country. They carry on continual guerrilla warfare against us."

Verano, Señor Ricardo revealed, was a stumbling block in the work of Hemispak.

"Why is that?" Tom asked.

"Our group is looking for undiscovered sources of uranium," he replied. "From a clue given by an old explorer, we believe that there is valuable radio-active material on the border of Verano. But it must not get into the hands of these rebels!" Ricardo cried.

"Would they know what to do with it?" Tom questioned.

"*Sí, sí*. They would sell it to a power hostile to the Americas. This we must prevent!"

"These rebels—they must be more than ordinary guerrillas," Mr. Swift remarked.

"They are cruel, ruthless men." Señor Ricardo looked grim. "Hemispak sent an expedition of scientists to the border, but we fear they have met with foul play from the rebels. It has been two weeks since we have heard from them by radio."

"Dad! That's probably the same expedition John Roberts is with!"

"What? You are acquainted with John Roberts?" Señor Ricardo asked in surprise. "He is one of Hemispak's finest scientists."

Mr. Swift explained how they knew him. "His father works for us. We've known John since his boyhood. This is indeed bad news."

"But you will not mention my worries to the father?"

"No," Mr. Swift agreed, but a frown creased his forehead. Roberts probably would learn it soon enough himself.

"They are good men, our scientific party," Ricardo was saying, "and it is very strange that we have had no word from them in so long a time. At this very moment those rebels may be forcing Roberts and the others to locate the uranium for them!"

"But you don't think the scientists will do it?" Tom said.

Señor Ricardo waved his hands in a gesture of despair. "How long can they hold out?" He leaned forward in his chair. "It all leads up to a very important question which I am about to ask you.

"Will you and your father help us thwart these dangerous rebels?"

Chapter V

ESPIONAGE

TOM'S EYES gleamed with eagerness as he waited a moment for his father's reply to the South American's question. This could be a high adventure!

"We need the help of you Swifts and your wonderful inventions," continued Señor Ricardo as he pressed his case, "both to locate our missing scientists and to investigate the presence of uranium deposits."

"I'd like to do it!" Tom cried. "What do you think, Dad?"

Mr. Swift, more cautious, asked whether Ricardo's government had tried to find the scientists.

"Yes, but we have not succeeded," the South American replied. "We believe if someone from a North American country came there the rebels would not—what you say—catch on."

Tom was more eager than ever to go. He wanted to rescue John Roberts before the man might be tortured into working for the rebels!

"Our answer depends upon how soon we would have to start," Mr. Swift said. "Tom and I have commitments to keep us here a couple of weeks. In that time a lot can happen in Verano."

"*Es verdad!* It is true!" their caller agreed. "I will keep you informed, of course. But I am sure our scientists will not give in to the rebels and help them find the uranium before then. They will hold out as long as they can."

"You mean, they won't give in until they're forced to," said Tom.

Ricardo nodded. "I shudder to think of those five scientists being tortured into helping the enemy. And now, I beg of you to accept my proposition."

Mr. Swift, after a few moments of further reflection, finally said, "We'll do all we can to assist you, though we won't promise complete success. That's a big assignment you've given us, Señor Ricardo!"

"But not too big," Tom spoke up, as the South American thanked them effusively. "And," the young inventor added, "in the Flying Lab with our new Geiger counter——"

"Ah, the enthusiasm of youth!" Ricardo beamed. "*Magnifico!* And now, one other request. Hemispak would be pleased to have both of you address our members at a meeting in Riverton day after tomorrow. Would you be so kind as to give us brief speeches on the latest technical developments—perhaps your new inventions? I assure you that all data will be held in strictest confidence."

Though Tom and his father usually refrained from speech-making to escape the publicity, they accepted because of their high regard for the work the Hemispak Scientific Society was doing. Señor Ricardo thanked them, then said:

"Before I go, I should like to see the Flying Lab you will fly to my country."

Tom felt that the Flying Lab was not ready to be exhibited. However, because of Ricardo's scientific position, the young inventor decided to give him a preview of the plane.

Ricardo's reaction was both amazing and amusing. After his first voluble praise, he seemed at a loss for words. But finally he murmured:

"It is *esplendido*! I have taken too much of your time already. I must leave."

As the Swifts walked to the main gate with him, he remarked, "I suggest one precaution. In future conversations between us let us use the nickname which Hemispak has for my country. If the Verano rebels should learn of your trip, I am sure they will cause more trouble. We will refer to my country only as Bapcho."

Señor Ricardo shook hands and left.

Tom turned to his father. "We'll have to speed up work here, that's sure, especially on the counter."

"Right. This trip will give it a real test," Mr. Swift answered. "Well, I'll see you at supper."

As Tom neared the underground hangar, he met Chow.

"Jumpin' sunspots!" Tom exclaimed as the good-natured cook approached, wearing a purple-and-orange plaid shirt.

"You like it, eh?" Chow asked.

"It's enough to start a stampede."

"Well, I dunno," Chow replied, stroking his chin and gazing at the breast pocket of Tom's jacket. "You seem to like colours, yourself. How about those red, green, an' blue pencils you're carryin'? Somethin' new for your draftin' board?"

"No," Tom said, pulling out the pencil-like objects. "I've had these awhile. This green one is a miniature radio. It will send and receive signals."

"Well, brand my balky ole mule!" the Texan exclaimed admiringly as he turned it over in his hand.

"An' these, I guess, are the secret buttons to turn it on."

"Right. The red pencil is a soldering iron that works by a tiny battery. Good for repairing electrical connections in a hurry. The blue pencil is a secret infrared snooperscope."

"For spottin' people in the dark?" Chow asked, scratching his head.

"You guessed it."

"Wow!" Chow exclaimed. "You're a one-man patent office!"

During the next two days, father and son applied themselves rigorously to a demanding and accelerated schedule of work. On the evening of the Hemispak meeting they drove to Riverton, parked near the building where the scientific seminar was to be held, and took the elevator to the fourth floor.

"I'm delighted to see you again," Señor Ricardo greeted them at the auditorium door.

As Tom was introduced to various members of the organization, he recognized many names as those of men he had heard about since childhood. Each was a leader in some scientific field.

A few minutes later Señor Ricardo opened the meeting. A look of expectancy came over the audience as he introduced Tom. Never before had the members been addressed by so young a scientist.

They listened intently as Tom told of plans for a trip to South America in the Swifts' new flying laboratory to look for uranium. When he said they were perfecting an invention to detect it from great heights —which was the most feasible method to use in high mountains—there was loud applause.

"There's an old Indian legend," Tom went on, "about

an Andes tribe which discovered a spot they named Devil's Canyon. Plants of unusual species found there grew to a fantastic size. Birds and even insects never visited it.

"The canyon contained a beautiful, clear stream which appeared magically from a cave in the mountainside. The Indians insisted that the cave glowed in the dark. They also said that to drink the water caused almost immediate baldness and brought on grave illness."

As a few enthusiastic *si si's* indicated that others in the audience also had heard the story, Tom continued:

"My own theory about this is that the water travels through radio-active ore deep in the mountain—say at least eighteen hundred feet down. If we want to locate this valuable deposit we'll need a super-Geiger counter. That's the chief reason why right now we're speeding up work on this new invention."

When Tom had related as much of his plans as he thought prudent, he concluded his talk with wishes of success for the Bapcho project. Loud handclapping and cheers followed as he took his seat.

Mr. Swift, who was introduced next, was greeted with equal enthusiasm. He immediately held his audience spellbound by revealing that a strange object from space had crashed into his airfield.

"We could have called it a meteorite and let it go at that. But it seemed to have a precise, machined shape. We made some test borings and analysed them in the mass spectrograph. The bulk of the object is a metal alloy of an isotopic composition not found on earth, and it has an external protective non-metallic sheath. This fused coating has thus far resisted our attempts to analyse it."

The man started furtively toward the exit

While his father was speaking, Tom suddenly noticed someone rise up from behind a row of seats near the back of the auditorium. As the man started furtively toward the exit, Tom gasped. He was the same slick-haired young man who had knocked him out at the spare-parts shed!

Tom left the platform quietly and slipped down the side aisle. But outside the auditorium, he broke into a run, down the corridor, after his quarry.

Clang!

The metallic clatter of the self-service elevator told him that the fugitive had started for the ground floor. Tom dashed for the stairway, leaping down it three steps at a time. He reached the bottom seconds after the echo of the opening elevator door reverberated up the shaft. He had missed his man!

Tom's eyes roved over the dimly lighted area from the doorway and he listened intently. There was not a sign of the man he was after.

A search along the street proved equally fruitless. Disappointed, Tom headed back to the meeting and reached it just in time to hear his father's concluding remarks.

As Tom took his place on the platform his mind was in a whirl. What use would the dark-haired stranger make of the information he had picked up?

As Señor Ricardo brought the meeting to a close, Mr. Swift came over to his son. "Did you go after that man I noticed hurrying out?" he asked.

"Yes, but he sure made a fast getaway! Dad, he was the fellow who slugged me and stole part of the Geiger plans. And now—he was spying here!"

When Señor Ricardo heard about the man's strange actions, he exclaimed, "A spy? But how could he have been admitted by the doorman?"

"He must have shown a fake membership card," Tom said. "We'd better alert the police."

"*Si, si!*" Señor Ricardo begged. "This is most serious!"

"Indeed it is," Mr. Swift agreed. "You phone the police, Tom, then we must start for home."

Tom made the call, suggesting that the suspect might live near by, since he had disappeared so quickly. Then the Swifts said goodbye to their Hemispak friends and, with Tom at the wheel, made the return trip to Shopton.

"I don't like this business," the older inventor said. "There's undoubtedly a lot more to the Verano affair than has come out."

"You mean, Dad, the men leading the rebels are playing for big stakes but aren't telling their plans to the small fellows?"

"Exactly. After they get the prize, they'll pull out. In the meantime, these Verano schemers will use any method to gain what they want—no matter how ruthless."

"All the more reason for us to complete our work."

The next morning at breakfast Mr. Swift said he was eager to start for his office to attack the problem of the Geiger counter and asked Tom if he was ready to go.

"I promised Uncle Ned," Tom replied, "that I'd give the *Pigeon Special* a good workout this morning. He's about ready to announce the new commuters' plane to the public and wants me to see whether I can set it down in somebody's driveway!"

Sandy, who was an excellent pilot, asked if she might fly with Tom, saying that she hoped some day to demonstrate the plane herself to prospective customers.

"Sure. Come along," Tom said. "You can take the *Pigeon* up and do a few stunts. I'll bring her down."

Twenty minutes later they reached the old Swift Construction Company, now an aircraft manufacturing centre. Mr. Ned Newton, a lifelong friend of Mr. Swift, was in charge. Mechanics rolled out the sleek propeller-driven two-seater, and Sandy took it up in a long, graceful arc.

"You're doing very well, Sis," Tom complimented her, after she had skilfully executed a series of S turns without skidding. "Try some simple stunts. But you'd better get more altitude first," he warned her. "Never do acrobatics with a ship too close to the ground!"

Sandy immediately eased back on the stick, and the small plane quickly rose another thousand feet.

"Here goes a loop." Then, mimicking her brother's voice, she said, "You fly straight and level as you start, then dive a little to pick up speed, and give it some left rudder. As you climb into the loop you add throttle, and at the top of the loop you ease the throttle back."

Tom grinned as the *Pigeon* whipped up and over in a creditable loop.

"Now try a barrel roll," he said.

Sandy puckered her lips, then said, "Chum, a barrel roll is just a simple turn, except that you keep the ship turning until it's upside down and back again. Here goes."

"Wait a minute!" Tom ordered. "Pull the stick back until the nose is just above the horizon. Then use——"

But Sandy had pulled the stick back too far, and the *Pigeon* began to lose flying speed rapidly. As she moved the stick to the right, the plane vibrated, then stalled, and plunged earthward in a buffeting spin. Sandy caught her breath.

"I have it," Tom said quietly.

He kicked in the right rudder, snapped the stick forward, and came out of the spin in a long dive with five hundred feet to spare. Then he used the speed of his dive to regain most of the altitude lost.

Sandy let out a sigh of relief. "That's enough barrel rolls for me," she said.

"Oh, no," Tom told her. "Try it again right now, or you'll never want to. Just don't pull the nose up so far that you lose all of your flying speed. Go ahead."

This time the roll was perfectly timed, and Sandy's confidence was restored.

"I'll take over now," her brother said. "I wonder just how small a spot I can set the *Pigeon* down in!"

Using the standard approach pattern to the field, he eased in over the countryside. Gently the plane nosed down, until it was only six hundred feet above a small wooded area on one side of the field.

Suddenly there was a terrific impact against the bottom of the fuselage. Something ripped through the floor, whizzed upward between them, and passed through the roof of the cockpit. The *Pigeon* gave a tremendous lurch.

"Someone's firing at us!" Tom shouted.

Chapter VI

THE CLICKING DETECTOR

"WE'LL have to crash land, Sandy! Hang on!"

Only the fact that Tom Swift was an experienced pilot prevented a bad crack-up. As it was, he levelled off just in time to pancake on the runway without cracking up.

There was a sickening screech as the damaged under-carriage was ripped away. But the ill-fated plane skidded to a stop. Tom and his sister sat in stunned silence a couple of seconds, then he said:

"Are you all right, Sandy?"

"I think so. At least, I don't believe any bones are broken. How about you?"

"I'm okay."

With shaking fingers Sandy unfastened her safety belt and slipped out of the seat. Tom helped her from the plane and they surveyed the damage.

"It could have been a lot worse," he said thankfully. "If that wasn't a deliberate attempt to kill us, I miss my guess!"

"But why?" Sandy asked quaveringly, and then added, "By the same man who knocked you out?"

Tom shrugged. "At least by someone who doesn't want me to go to South America."

A crash truck roared up the runway with three crew members and Bud Barclay who had come over to drive Tom to the Enterprises plant.

"You two all right?" Bud cried out.

Tom nodded and explained what had happened, saying he believed an anti-aircraft bazooka had sent a rocket through the plane.

"What!" Bud exclaimed, as he examined the gashes in the floor and ceiling of the pilot's cabin. "Boy, if that thing had exploded——"

"The rocket launcher must have been in the woods," Tom declared. "I'm going over and investigate. Anybody want to come?"

Bud and all the crash crew joined him. Sandy, shaken by the experience, acceded to Tom's request that she drive home at once.

Tom's hope of finding the man soon faded. There was no sign of him in the woods, although the searchers looked thoroughly in the underbrush.

"Hey, wait a sec!" Bud yelled as they were about to leave. "This might be a clue to that bazooka man!"

He held up a plane schedule.

"From South America!" Tom cried. "If that man dropped this, then I'd say he's one of the rebels."

Bud snorted. "By my arithmetic, that's two attacks on you from those rebels. And two *too* many!"

"It certainly looks that way." Tom clenched his fists. "But when he shoots at Sandy——"

"Whatever you do to him, count me in on it," Bud growled. "Say, how do you figure they found out that you were going to test the *Pigeon* this morning?"

"I wish I knew," Tom said solemnly. "There must be a nest of spies around here."

"Well, for Pete's sake, watch your step!" Bud urged.

On the way to the Enterprises plant the boys talked of nothing else but the attack. And when Tom told his father about it, Mr. Swift looked grave.

"This is really cause for alarm," he said. "Until we get to the bottom of it, you must be extra cautious, Tom. Better report this incident to the police at once."

"I'll do that, and suggest they check on planes to South America, both public and private."

During his son's absence, Mr. Swift had been working on the super-Geiger counter. He now announced his satisfaction with the result of a new mixture of gases.

"Tomorrow we'll take the model up in a plane and try it on some buried uranium," he said.

The following morning, after Tom had finished an inspection of the altimeters on the Flying Lab, he drove to a spot far removed from the Swift Enterprises buildings where his father was directing some digging. Two workmen, operating a power boring drill, were sinking a hole deep in the ground.

"We're about ready to bury the uranium," Mr. Swift said. "I think the hole's deep enough. They're down twenty feet now."

He walked over to where a heavy lead cylinder lay in a cart. The cylinder contained two curies of a naturally occurring radio-active uranium isotope.

"All right, men," he said. "Remove the shield and lower this into the hole with the crane. I don't want any of you within fifty feet of this 'hot' uranium until after it's covered with dirt." When this was done, he turned to Tom. "We're ready."

"I'll get the cargo ship," his son said, and drove back to the hangar. The counter had already been hoisted aboard and secured.

"She's ready to go," the mechanic on duty informed him. "Just tuned her up. The engines sound sweet."

"Roger."

Tom taxied up the airstrip to where his father was waiting. Mr. Swift slid into the co-pilot's seat, and the plane started down the runway. In a matter of seconds they were airborne. Tom climbed steeply and then levelled off at two thousand feet.

"Let's try the counter at this low altitude first," he suggested.

Mr. Swift, agreeing, moved aft.

"Ready here," he called. "Give her a run."

Winging over the Swift Enterprises grounds, Tom eased the throttle. Presently the tell-tale *click-click* sounded in the counter, at first faintly, then in a pronounced steady series.

"Well, it works!" Mr. Swift chuckled.

"Let's try it at five thousand feet," Tom suggested as he put the plane into a steep climb.

At five thousand feet he levelled off once more, starting another run over the buried uranium. This time the clicking sounds came much less evenly and very weakly.

"But it's there!" Mr. Swift said as he tried to adjust the counter so that it would produce a firmer count.

"It's there, yes," Tom replied. "But will it work at say, ten thousand, where we'd normally be cruising?" He set his jaw. "We may as well find out now."

He pulled the ship into another upward surge. When the altimeter read ten thousand feet, Tom levelled off but the counter registered no sound other than the normal background clicking. Mr. Swift's face showed his keen disappointment.

"Our invention probably wouldn't detect radio-active particles buried deep in the ground," he said. "There must be some way to improve the counter, though. Maybe an entirely new approach to the problem."

As Tom set the big ship down in a feather-touch landing, he exclaimed, "That's it, Dad! A new approach. We must throw out present-day methods."

A few moments later he cried, "I have an idea! A completely new scheme!"

Chapter VII

SKY RACERS

ARRIVING at the main office with his father, Tom found a telegram for him from Washington. It said that Ripcord Hulse was arriving for the first flight of the *Sky Queen,* and would land at the old Swift field the following afternoon about two-thirty.

"Wow!" Tom cried. "That doesn't give us much time to get the Flying Lab ready for her initial hop."

Mr. Swift smiled. "A lot can be done in a few hours if everyone gets busy," he said. "Rip's not interested in the laboratory equipment, so that can wait until after the test."

Tom hurried off to the underground hangar to check on what still had to be done before the big plane could take off. Everything seemed to be progressing satisfactorily with one exception. Finding that the engineer in charge of the electric compass was having difficulty calibrating it, Tom worked with him for an hour until it registered accurately.

"Now I guess we won't have any trouble with it," he said, and then went off to look for Bud. Finding his friend in the plant's restaurant, he said:

"Rip's flying in tomorrow. I want to give the *Kangaroo Kub* and the *Skeeter* another good work-out before they're put aboard the Flying Lab. How about a race? You take the copter and I'll fly the plane. I'll give you a ten-minute start."

"You're on, jet jockey!" Bud agreed, swallowing the last of an ice-cream soda.

Side by side the boys warmed up the two flying "babies." Then Tom called out:

"We'll make a ten-mile run to the yacht club, wing over, fly back above the construction company field, and circle back above the high school."

"And finish up with a precision landing between those two big poplar trees at the edge of the woods," Bud shouted back. "Let's see who comes closer to this line." He pointed to a tar strip in the runway. "I'll bet on Bud Barclay."

"So you think you can beat me in that windmill," Tom jibed.

"Windmill!" Bud exploded. "What do you think this is, one of those paddle-wheel river boats?"

"No, just a Swift egg beater," Tom called. Bud mumbled something Tom could not hear, as he revved up the special elevator and flying engines of the helicopter. A few moments afterward he left the ground with surprising speed.

Ten minutes later Tom's plane took off with a *whoosh*. Though Bud had zipped along the course in good time, Tom overtook him in a matter of minutes. He picked up his mike and switched to the private wavelength.

"Hey, Bud. Bet I'll be back at the field working on those mysterious symbols before you're half-way around the course," he told the co-pilot. "Roger. Out."

As Tom reached the yacht club, over which he was to make the first turn, he started to ease the aileron and rudder. Suddenly he realized that something was wrong. The rudder was jammed—so much so that he could make only a very slight turn.

"I'll be lucky to get back at all!" he muttered, considerably worried.

Carefully Tom banked the tiny plane as sharply as he could. It responded sluggishly, and in order to complete the turn, he had to cover several extra miles on that leg of the trip.

He experienced the same difficulty at the other turns of the impromptu pre-arranged race course. Arriving finally at the Swift Enterprises airstrip, Tom saw the *Skeeter* on the ground. Bud walked over to the *Kangaroo Kub*, raised his eyebrows, and glanced at his friend.

"Well, fly boy, want to sell your jet cheap and buy a windmill?" he asked.

Grinning ruefully, Tom related his discomfiting experience with the jammed rudder. Concerned, Bud helped him examine the plane. They quickly found that a loose wire had tangled with other rudder control wires and caused the jam. Working together, it did not take them long to correct the trouble.

"Now, I'll give you another chance," Bud proposed. "After all, that wasn't much of a speed test."

Once again the two craft started on the course. This time Tom flipped the *Kangaroo Kub* sharply around the turns. Shooting far out in front on the first leg, he lost sight of Bud on the second, and whipped quickly in from the third and last stretch.

When Bud finally brought the *Skeeter* back to earth, Tom was waiting for him with a look of exaggerated triumph on his face.

"Been away?" he asked, showing Bud a series of equations and formulas he had been making on a pad. "I've had a lot of time to work on these space symbols."

Bud gave him a shove. "Listen, I'll admit I can't beat your plane for pure speed, but I'll take this little number any time." He patted the helicopter's fuselage.

After checking the speeds of both aircraft, Tom was well pleased with their performance. "I guess that about winds up our work on them," he remarked. "All we have to do now is install them inside the Flying Lab."

Tom and Bud went at once to check the tie lines and blocks in the Flying Lab that would hold the planes fast. As they finished, Bud yawned.

"Say, Tom, how'd you make out with those symbols?"

"No new developments, and Dad hasn't solved the mystery either."

When the boys came outdoors, Bud looked up into space. "Isn't Mars in that direction?" he asked, pointing. "Bet you a bunch of scientific gnomes are sitting up there on the other planet laughing their heads off at us."

"You could be right," Tom agreed. "But some professors think Martians are giants."

During the next morning, the necessary finishing touches for a successful flight were put on the Flying Lab. As Tom and his father inspected the result, the two inventors smiled. Then Tom sobered.

"There's one thing we'll have to do before we can take the *Sky Queen* into the upper stratosphere or ionosphere," he said. "We can't risk the danger of being irradiated with cosmic rays."

"That's true, son. The wild blue yonder no doubt contains more surprises than the Flying Lab is prepared to meet at this moment."

"What do you think of covering the entire exterior and interior with Tomasite?" Tom asked.

"A splendid idea," Mr. Swift said approvingly. "The extra weight will be negligible."

"I'll attend to it at once," Tom replied, and gave orders for this to be done.

After lunch the Swifts drove with Bud to the airfield at the old construction company to meet Ripcord Hulse, now in the Army Intelligence Service. Presently they heard the familiar, high-pitched whine of a jet engine overhead.

"There's Rip!" Tom cried as the ship whistled over the field and started to turn back in a long, easy arc.

"He'll be down in a couple of minutes now," Bud said eagerly.

Suddenly Tom gripped his friend's arm. "Look! Something's happened!" he cried.

All they could see was a blinding flash from the spot where the big jet had last been visible. Seconds later a loud *boom* followed the flash.

The ship had exploded!

Chapter VIII

MIDNIGHT GENIUS

SPEECHLESS, Tom, his father and Bud stared at the sky.

"There's a chute! It just opened!" Tom shouted. "He's coming down in the woods!"

With a rush, the three observers jumped into the car and raced out past the startled guards at the entrance.

"He can't be more than half a mile away," Bud said tensely as they sped over the uneven country road.

"I'm afraid Rip may be in bad shape," Tom said anxiously. "I wonder if his plane had one of those projectile seats that shoot out automatically at a blast."

"We can only hope that he missed the worst of it," replied Mr. Swift.

Tom, peering anxiously ahead, spun the car expertly around the curves toward the area where the chute had fallen. "Rip must have landed somewhere along here," he said, turning off the road and swinging bumpily down a narrow lane.

They skirted the edge of a meadow, looking intently among the trees that lined the road.

"There he is!" Bud exclaimed, pointing across the field. "Dangling in that tree!"

From where they were, the three could distinguish a man, swaying from one of the trees on the edge of the open expanse, about fifteen feet off the ground. Mr. Swift whipped a first-aid kit from the dashboard compartment, as the boys leaped from the car and ran to aid the pilot.

"It's Rip Hulse, all right!" Tom exclaimed.

The pilot hung suspended by the shroud lines of a parachute. Its canopy was caught fast in the top-most branches. Looking up, the others could see a smear of blood across the airman's face, and his right arm hung crookedly. Though conscious, Hulse was still dazed, for he stared at them as if not fully aware that help had arrived.

"We'll get you down," Tom called up to him.

Quickly he and Bud clambered up the tree to a position above Rip. With a firm grip on him they severed the cords from the main body of the chute, then carefully lowered him. Mr. Swift eased the pilot to the ground.

By this time, Ripcord Hulse was regaining his wits. Perspiration streamed down his face and he was obviously in great pain.

"My shoulder . . ." he said falteringly, "dislocated . . . always happens . . . like a trick knee. Pull the arm straight out for me . . ."

Tom jumped forward to help. Gently he exerted pressure on the flier's injured arm until there was a sudden relief of tension, and the arm snapped back into the shoulder socket. There was a gasp from Rip, then a smile of thanks.

"This is a fine way for me to arrive for a visit," he said, sitting up.

"Never mind that. I'm glad you're safe," Tom replied.

Mr. Swift introduced Bud, then examined the cut on Rip's cheekbone. Satisfied that it was not a bad injury, he applied antiseptic and then placed a patch on it.

As Ripcord tried to stand up, one leg gave way. Tom and Bud grabbed him.

"We're taking you straight to the hospital," said Mr. Swift.

The boys leaped from the car and ran to aid the pilot

"Guess I can't make it at that," the pilot said. "But before we go, let's take a look at the wreckage for evidence of sabotage."

"Sabotage?" Tom repeated. "Do you think that was the cause of the explosion?"

Rip's face darkened, and his wide generous mouth became a thin line.

"I'm afraid so. Ever since I was given the job of trailing a suspicious A.W.O.L. Air Force pilot, I've run into trouble. I think a bomb was placed on board."

The boys gathered the deflated chute, then went in search of pieces of the plane. They found them about half a mile away, scattered over a wide area.

"It's going to be tough for the FBI to find any evidence of sabotage," Tom commented.

Bud kicked at a couple of the smaller remnants of the once sleek jet and remarked wryly, "Even those brainy boys'll have a tough time figuring anything out of bits like these!"

On the way to the hospital Mr. Swift telephoned news of the disaster to the FBI. He also asked that the local police have a man guard the debris.

Meanwhile, Tom had been giving Rip a description of the *Sky Queen*. The ace's eyes lighted in anticipation of the initial test. Then suddenly he remembered his injuries.

"But I can't hold you up," he said. "I don't know how long this leg'll keep me in the hospital. I hope it isn't fractured."

Tom told him that they would gladly hold up the test a few days. "Let us know what the doctor says."

A few hours later the flier phoned that the injury to his leg was not so serious as he had thought and he would be ready for the test flight three days later.

"Good," said Tom. "We'll wait."

In the meantime, Tom again examined the hoists for the mammoth elevator that would raise the *Sky Queen* to ground level. He decided that one of the compressor motors should be stepped up. After leaving orders for this to be done, Tom heaved a sigh of relief. Now he could concentrate on the uranium-detector idea.

A few minutes later Bud found him in the underground hangar office drawing a sketch on the back of an envelope.

"What's that?" he asked.

"My latest brain storm," Tom replied.

"About what?"

"A novel idea for a long-range radio-activity detector."

"How is it novel?" Bud asked.

Tom ran his fingers through his already rumpled hair. "This gets away from the Geiger counter idea completely. I'm going to our optical lab to work on it. Want to come?"

"Lead the way, genius," Bud answered. "If this is the birth of something big, I want to be in on it."

"You'd better plan to spend some long hours at it," Tom told him.

"I'll help," Bud declared loyally.

The two boys made their way to a small cubicle of the Flying Lab which had only recently been furnished. Inside was a long bench, equipped with callipers, grinding wheels and tools, and a wide assortment of prisms and lenses.

Tom switched on a bright light, then opened a wall cabinet containing some new equipment which Bud had not seen. He whistled in surprise.

"Boy! What photographic equipment! Are you going to take pictures? I thought you were working on a detector."

c

"I am," Tom said with a smile. "Photography will be part of the invention."

"Now look, Tom," Bud said sceptically, "don't tell me you intend to take a picture of a radio-active wave!"

Tom was so busy adjusting a large lens that he did not hear the question. Bud followed his friend to the workbench and repeated the query.

"You're on the right track," Tom replied.

Tom's hands worked with dexterity as he went about his task, whistling softly to himself. This was proof to Bud that everything was working out to the inventor's satisfaction.

The co-pilot watched in growing wonder for nearly an hour as Tom worked methodically on what resembled a large, old-fashioned box camera, which was two feet square and made of heavy metal.

"For the love of aerodynamics, Tom," Bud said, finally unable to restrain his curiosity any longer, "just what are you doing?"

Without pausing in his work or looking up from the bench, Tom replied, "Know what happens in nuclear decomposition?"

"Yes. Radiation."

"Right. Then what?"

Bud scratched his head. "I give up. What?"

"It produces fluorescence in neighbouring molecules. Like making watch hands glow in the dark."

"At this point I'm completely lost in a cloud bank," Bud admitted.

Tom's hands ceased their activity for a moment and he stared straight ahead, as if looking through space.

"Now, a bed of uranium ore won't glow in the dark," Tom continued, as if visualizing the complete invention, "but I'm going to try constructing a photometer with non-absorptive prisms. With it we might be able to detect fluorescence from considerable distances, and record its density on photographic film. Bring me a roll of motion-picture film from cabinet C, will you, please?"

Bud marvelled at the rapid-fire functioning of his friend's mind. Getting the film, he took it to the workbench, where Tom fitted it into the contraption.

"Say, pal, it's way past supper-time," Bud reminded him.

"Well, how about getting us some sandwiches and milk? And phone Mother that I might not be home tonight, will you?"

"Hey, Tom, have a heart. You want me to starve to death?"

"Suit yourself, but bring me some food," Tom said, slapping his friend on the shoulder.

Bud went off, returning presently with double portions for both of them. At three o'clock the next morning light still glowed in the optical laboratory. Inside, Tom Swift, his collar open and his tie loosened, was drilling screw holes in the black box.

"This just about does it, Bud," he said excitedly. "Hey, Bud! Wake up! You're a fine assistant!"

Seated on a stool beside Tom, his head resting on his arms, Bud Barclay was snoring gently.

"Huh? What did you say, Tom?"

"I said wake up. This radio-activity detector is nearly finished. Grab a handful of two-inch metal screws and set them just where I've drilled these holes."

A half-hour later Tom stood back from the black box.

"This is it, Bud," he said. "If my invention works, it will detect uranium in those South American mountains no matter how deep it's buried!"

Chapter IX

GHOSTLY PHOTOS

"SOUNDS TERRIFIC, Tom!" Bud said. "When do we try out your midnight brain storm?"

"After we catch forty winks."

"That I'm glad to hear!" Bud yawned. Tom smiled because his friend had had forty winks every hour since eleven o'clock.

"I figure on taking the detector up for a test about ten o'clock tomorrow—what am I saying—I mean, this morning."

"It's today, all right!" Bud agreed as he rose slowly from his stool. "When I'm working on an invention with you, pal, I hardly know whether it's today, tomorrow, or yesterday!"

Tom laughed. "Guess we'd better call it quits before we both start walking home in our sleep!"

As they started for the door, Tom suddenly stopped and grabbed Bud's arm.

"Hey!" he almost yelled. "Of all things to forget——"

Bud groaned, sure that his friend had been struck with some new idea for improving the invention and would insist upon staying to complete it.

"Don't worry," said Tom. "I'm only going to call Roberts over here to watch this detector. You go ahead and wait for me in the car. Be with you in a second."

He switched on the intercom.

"Calling Mr. Roberts. Please come to the optical lab at once. This is Tom."

Two minutes later the custodian arrived somewhat out of breath.

"There's a valuable piece of equipment here," Tom told him. "I want it closely guarded."

"A new invention, Tom?" Roberts asked, glancing at the black box. "You won't have to worry. I'll post one guard in this room and another outside the building."

Tom grabbed his jacket and hastened off to join Bud. When they arrived at the Swift home a few minutes later, he hopped out of the car.

"See you at ten," he called.

"Sure thing! *Adios* for now."

Tom fell into a deep sleep, awakening only in time for a late breakfast. He hurried to the Enterprises plant, going straight to the underground office where he hoped to find his father. Mr. Swift looked up from the map of South America he had been studying.

"Well, son! Didn't expect to see you awake till this afternoon. Did you stay up long to work on that latest inspiration of yours?"

"Yes, just about. But it was worth every minute of the time Bud and I spent, Dad!" Tom handed his father the rough plans from which he had worked. "The invention's finished—ready for its first test today."

"Incredible!" Mr. Swift said with a smile. "It's really a challenge to keep up with you these days, Tom."

"Will you come over and have a look at my apparatus?"

Mr. Swift had already risen from his chair and was striding eagerly toward the door. "Let's go. You can brief me about the details on the way."

By the time they reached the optical laboratory, Tom

had given his father a concise description of his uranium detector.

"Sounds all right, in theory," commented Mr. Swift, as one of the electronic keys opened the door. "However, it's hard to believe that your detector can measure up to, let alone surpass the Geiger counter that took the foremost inventors so many years to perfect."

"I don't blame you for being a bit doubtful, Dad, when I spent only a little over twelve hours working out mine. But I've been thinking about it for days."

They were greeted by Roberts who said he had stood guard over the invention since the boys had left the laboratory.

"Thanks a lot," Tom smiled appreciatively.

After Roberts had departed, Tom asked his father, who had been closely examining the black box, what he thought of it.

"Tom, I'm trying not to be over-enthusiastic at this point," Mr. Swift said, "but at first glance, I would say that this could very well be a revolutionary instrument for locating uranium."

"Awfully glad to hear you say that," Tom said, pleased by his father's reaction. "But we'll know for sure pretty soon. Bud and I are going to try my detector in the cargo plane. Come with us, won't you?"

"Wouldn't miss it."

"Fine. I'll call the men at the outdoor hangar to warm up the engines. It's nearly ten o'clock. Bud will be here any minute."

"By the way," his father said, after Tom had phoned the mechanics, "have you thought of a name for your detector yet?"

"Yes, I have, Dad. You might think it's sentimental, but I'd like to honour our old friend Mr. Damon. I'll never forget him and his wonderful philosophy. He taught me lots of interesting things before he passed on. I'd like to make this a sort of memorial to him."

"That surely is a noble thought, Tom," said Mr. Swift, recalling vividly the likeable old gentleman who had encouraged him as a youth and had gone on many hazardous adventures with him.

"How does Damonscope sound to you?" Tom asked.

"Couldn't be better, son."

"I only hope it lives up to its name when we fly over the buried uranium."

At that moment Bud arrived, his eyes bright after a few hours' solid sleep. "I'm rarin' to take off with the black box, skipper," he announced cheerily to Tom. "Hello there, Mr. Swift."

"Glad to see you've recuperated from that all-night session." Mr. Swift smiled.

"We're all set," said Tom. "Dad's going along. Also, our invention has been christened the Damonscope."

"Say, that's good. After that old Mr. Damon you've both been talking about so much!"

"That's the idea, Bud. Let's carry the Damonscope out to the airstrip."

The two boys lifted the detector carefully, and accompanied by Mr. Swift, proceeded to the runway. The cargo plane had been rolled out and its engines were humming. Tom and Bud placed the Damonscope aboard, adjusting it so that its powerful lens protruded through an opening in the floor.

Bud went forward quickly and took his place at the controls. "Ready?" he called back.

"All set! Go ahead!" Tom answered. As the plane climbed skyward, he said to his father, "I want you to make the first test of the Damonscope."

"I'd like that very much," replied Mr. Swift.

Tom raised his voice. "Bud, you can take 'er over the buried uranium now."

"Roger, skipper. Here goes!" Climbing to ten thousand feet, Bud levelled off and then called through the intercom, "Ready? I'll make a run over the spot."

Mr. Swift pressed a button on the side of the Damonscope and the camera began to whir quietly. Bud made several passes over the buried target.

"Okay now," Tom said. "I can develop the film right in the Damonscope."

Mr. Swift watched as excitedly as his son until the film was ready, then Tom held it up to the light. On the moving strip of celluloid, not quite dry, could be seen unmistakeable evidence of exposure to ultra-violet fluorescence. It was most intense in the middle of the strip, indicating the instant when the camera had passed directly over the buried uranium.

"It works!" Tom cried.

Mr. Swift looked at his son in sincere admiration. "Congratulations, Tom!" he cried. Then with a chuckle he added, "To tell you the truth, I didn't think it would work—at least not without several major adjustments."

When Bud was told the good news, he gave a whoop, followed by a mock salute. "My hat's off to the young genius," he said. "Well, there's nothing to stop us now from beating the rebels to that South American uranium. When do we start?"

"As soon as possible," Mr. Swift answered. "By the time Ripcord is ready for the test flight, the Flying Lab will be fully equipped."

"If everything's okay on the test," Tom added, "it won't take us long to get to Verano, Bud. Wait till you see how the *Sky Queen* burns up the miles."

Bud landed and the Damonscope was put into a vault until it was ready to be installed in the big ship. Tom, his father, and Bud separated, in order to attend to their individual jobs. An hour later when Tom went to the office in the main building to phone Rip his father was there.

"I have news for you, son," he said. "First, the Riverton police called. They have a good lead on that fellow who attacked you and stole the *Skeeter*."

"That *is* news," Tom replied. "Where is he?"

"They don't know, but they said that at the time we were there he had a room near the auditorium. He moved out in a hurry.

"The other bit of news is a telegram from Señor Ricardo. He's sending a man named José Berg to work with us."

"To work with us?" Tom repeated. "Why?"

"To brief us on our difficult task in South America," Mr. Swift explained. "Also, Ricardo feels that we should become familiar with the terrain and the customs and the living conditions in Verano."

Tom smiled. "A short course in Bapcho history, eh?"

His father said the visitor was due to arrive some time that day.

"Call your mother, Tom, and tell her we may bring Señor Berg home to lunch," he requested.

Tom made the call, but before delivering the message, he said, "Mother, the new invention works! And I'm going to call it the Damonscope."

"That's wonderful, dear! I'm so happy for you!"

"Is Sandy there?" Tom asked. He wanted to be the first to tell his sister.

"No. She went horseback riding with Phyl, but they'll be back by noon."

Phyllis Newton, daughter of Ned Newton, was Sandy's closest friend. Like Sandy, she was an enthusiastic horsewoman.

"Did you warn Sandy not to go on any back roads again?" Tom asked.

"Yes. She promised to stay on the well-travelled bridle paths."

Tom told of the luncheon plans, then hung up. He had barely put down the phone when Miss Trent called to say Señor Berg was there to see the Swifts.

"He didn't lose any time," Tom commented.

The two Swifts stood up to greet their caller who wore heavy tortoise-shell rimmed glasses.

"So happy to meet you," said the young man, his expansive smile revealing exceptionally glistening teeth.

"I am Señor José Berg of the Hemispak Scientific Society, and I bring with me a letter of introduction from our president, Carlos Ricardo."

First Mr. Swift, then Tom, shook hands with him. As Mr. Swift accepted the note and read it, Tom studied their visitor. He did not recall having seen him at the Hemispak meeting.

"You were not at the meeting?" he observed, offering the man a chair.

"Meeting? What meeting?" Mr. Berg asked.

"The Hemispak meeting at which my father and I spoke."

"Oh, that one! Why, no. As a matter of fact, I hadn't arrived in your country at that time."

Mr. Swift, who had finished reading the note, remarked, "Señor Ricardo suggested we should become better acquainted, Mr. Berg. He says you can be of great assistance in preparing us for what lies ahead."

"And you, in return"—beamed their visitor, his expansive smile even broader—"have so much scientific data that I would like to learn about. I also am eager to see the Flying Lab, and the other inventions about which Hemispak members have heard so much."

Tom listened to the man with a growing sense of uneasiness. The young inventor did not know exactly why, but he was sure of one thing: he would want to know Señor Berg a lot better before revealing any of the Swifts' valuable researches.

During a lull in the conversation, Tom said, "That idea of using a nickname for your country is a very clever one."

"Nickname?" Señor Berg frowned.

"Tom means a word to take the place of the real name," Mr. Swift explained.

"Oh, *si, si,* you mean—Bapcho!"

Tom relaxed. Apparently his suspicions concerning the stranger had been groundless. As his father gave him a knowing smile, the private telephone on Tom's desk rang.

"Tom! Thank goodness I found you!" his mother's relieved voice came over the wire.

"Why? Is something wrong?" Tom spoke very low.

"It's Sandy—Jumper came home without her!" Mrs. Swift's voice trembled with anxiety. "Don't say anything to your father yet, Tom, but I'm frantic with worry because we—we've been threatened!"

Chapter X

A THREAT COMES TRUE

"I'LL COME at once!" Tom assured his mother.

Hastily excusing himself, he hurried from the office. Half-way to the private entrance, he spotted Bud Barclay coming out of one of the hangars.

He shouted to him, and when Bud ran up, relayed his mother's message.

"I may need your help. Come along," he said.

Together, they sprinted to where Bud's car was parked, calling to the guard to open the gates.

"If Sandy's been hurt——" Tom looked grim as he considered the possibilities.

Bud clenched his fists. "Just let me get my hands on anybody who——"

The convertible roared along the road as he gave it full power. Mrs. Swift was waiting for them in front of the house, as the car shrieked to an abrupt halt. Her attractive, usually calm face was troubled and Tom knew that she was trying hard to hold back tears.

"Don't worry, Mother. We'll find Sandy," he said. "Who threatened us?"

"Some strange man. He telephoned right after Sandy rode off. He wouldn't give his name, but he said in a rough voice:

"'You were warned not to pursue our man. Call off the police at once!'"

"Good night!" Bud exclaimed.

"Was that all?" Tom asked.

"No." His mother went on: "He said that if the police got any hotter on their trail, all the Swifts would suffer for it!"

Tom realized that the police at that very moment *were hot on the trail*! Did their enemies plan to retaliate by kidnapping Sandy? Could she be their prisoner at this very moment?

"Mother, you said Phyl was with her. Is she missing too?"

"No, Phyl's home. I phoned her. She left Sandy at the flying field over an hour ago. I checked, but she's not there now. What'll we do?"

Before Tom could answer, he saw Phyl Newton hurrying up the walk. Her pretty face was flushed, and her dark hair was blowing wildly in the breeze.

"What's happened to Sandy?" she cried.

"We don't know," Mrs. Swift answered. "When you left her at the airfield, didn't she say what she was going to do?"

"No, but I'm sure Sandy didn't plan to fly," Phyl replied. "Maybe——"

"Yes?" Tom asked.

"I just remembered Sandy said that some time she was going to stop at our old riding master's house on Parker Lane. Maybe that's where she went."

A phone call to his house revealed that Sandy had indeed been there but had left over half an hour before. He said she had taken the Stony Brook bridle path toward home.

"Oh," said Mrs. Swift, "Sandy may be lying injured along the trail!"

"We'll soon find out!" Tom cried, and rushed from the house with Bud at his heels.

Phyl insisted upon going along and dashed after them. She hopped in the car and a few minutes later they passed the riding master's house.

Reaching the narrow Stony Brook bridle path which ran through a wood, they noticed the tracks of a car which had started in but had been forced to back out of the narrow opening. Tom parked and they all started down the path. There were hundreds of hoofprints. It was impossible to tell which ones had been made by Sandy's horse.

"Sandy! Sandy!" Tom shouted.

When there was no response, the searchers started running along the trail. Fifteen minutes later they came to the end of it without having found any sign of Sandy.

"Stymied!" Bud muttered. "What's our next move?"

After a conference it was decided that Phyl would cut cross lots, then walk along the road toward the Swift home, and report to them if she had found any trace of Sandy. Meanwhile, the boys would comb the woods, each taking one side of the trail. Every ten minutes they would meet to report progress.

"After that threat," Bud said, starting off, "you don't really think Sandy's around here, do you?"

Tom shrugged. "Anything could have happened. I'm just hoping she wasn't kidnapped."

Bud winced at this possibility. Tom himself tried not to dwell on the idea as he hunted through the under-brush. Twice the boys met at the trail without having found a trace of the missing girl.

"There's only one more section to search," Bud said, a note of hopelessness creeping into his voice.

"But I'm not stopping here," Tom declared. "I'm not giving up until I've covered every inch of this county if necessary."

"Phyl hasn't come back, so we know that she didn't find Sandy," Bud remarked, his face revealing his anxiety.

Minutes later, as Tom neared the area where they had parked the car, he suddenly stopped.

"Those broken bushes!" he exclaimed. "And those hoofmarks—a horse must have gone wild here!"

Cupping his hands, he shouted for Bud, bringing the co-pilot on the dead run.

Some distance in from the bridle path low bushes had been crushed and the earth kicked up. A man's deep footprints mingled with the hoofmarks.

"There's more trampled underbrush over there." Tom pointed as he pressed into the thickly overgrown section. "Bud! Look! It's Sandy!"

The girl was bound to the trunk of a young tree, a gag in her mouth. Quickly Tom whipped away the thick, coarse handkerchief while Bud untied the ropes.

"Oh, Tom!" she cried, throwing her arms around him. "Thanks a million, Bud."

"Sis, are you all right?" Tom asked anxiously as she sagged in his arms.

Sandy was almost too weak to talk. But she nodded, and the boys could see that she was more frightened than hurt.

They helped her to a flat rock near the edge of the trail where she sat down. Using a large leaf, Bud made a cup and brought her a drink of spring water.

"If you feel like talking now, Sis," Tom said, after she had sipped the water, "we'd like to find out exactly what happened."

"I'm all right," Sandy answered, breathing more normally. "But that awful man and woman——"

"Start at the beginning," Tom urged.

"All right. I'd just ridden into the woods when I noticed a car behind me. It came right onto the trail and almost bumped into my horse! He went wild and bolted off among the trees."

"Then what?" Bud prompted as Sandy paused.

"Then a man and a woman got out of the car and came after me. I tried to make Jumper gallop away from them, but he was still frightened and reared and went in circles."

"That gave the man a chance to pull you off the horse," Tom prompted.

"Yes, and Jumper ran away."

"He's home," Tom told her. "What happened then?"

"They tied my hands and bound me to a tree. When I started to shout for help, they gagged me. I could hardly breathe."

"They'll pay for this!" Tom muttered. "Did they say why they were tying you up?"

"Oh, yes, the man said the Swifts had been warned about interfering in other people's business. You hadn't paid any attention to the warnings, and now the police were after a friend of theirs. He said maybe this would teach the Swifts a lesson."

"The rat!" Bud burst out. "I'll beat him to a pulp!"

"That dreadful woman was just as bad," Sandy went on. "She said no one would ever find me, and I would starve to death!"

"What do they look like?" Tom asked.

"The man is heavy set. Has a big face but a very small chin. Ugly looking, with eyes like a pig. I don't know what nationality."

"And the woman?"

Sandy stood up. "Tall, reddish hair, and freckles. Sort

of washed-out looking. I'm awfully tired, Tom. Let's go home."

"Pronto."

When they reached the house, Mrs. Swift and Phyl came running to meet them. They hugged Sandy and asked what had happened. After hearing the story, Mrs. Swift exclaimed:

"This must be reported at once! Tom, call headquarters."

The police captain, greatly concerned with this latest development in the Swift mystery, said he would come to the house personally to question Sandy about the details. While waiting for him, Sandy suddenly laughed.

"Mother, believe it or not, I'm hungry."

Tom, glancing at the clock, realized that his father and Señor Berg were quite late for lunch. Mrs. Swift, sensing his thoughts, suggested that Tom phoned his father. The inventor, like his son, sometimes became so absorbed in his work that he forgot about food.

"Hello, Miss Trent," Tom said. "Dad around?"

"He went to the Flying Lab some time ago with Mr. Berg," the secretary answered. "I'll see if he's there."

A mechanic on the Flying Lab said Mr. Swift was not there, and persistent ringing of the underground-office phone brought no response. A general inquiry throughout the plant did not reveal Mr. Swift's whereabouts, so finally Tom hung up.

After ten minutes had gone by, Tom became uneasy. Where was his father? The threat against the Swifts might have been carried out a second time!

In the family's town car Tom drove quickly to the plant and let himself into the underground hangar. He could hear hammering in the distance; otherwise, everything was quiet.

A quick glance into the office showed that his father was not there. Deciding to question the workmen, Tom climbed the steps to the first level of the *Sky Queen*, but no mechanics were there.

As Tom was about to ascend the inner stairway, he suddenly became aware of a persistent ticking noise nearby. A clock? But there was no mechanical clock in the *Sky Queen*. The only timepieces were noiseless electronic clocks of Tom's own design.

What was the ticking, anyway?

Tom's eyes swept the dimly lighted area. At first he could see nothing out of the ordinary. Then he sighted a small, round object. Quickly he leaped toward it.

One glance was enough to confirm his fears. A time bomb!

Chapter XI

SPY HUNT

TOM KNEW that he had to act fast. Snatching the bomb, he raced down the steps, noting that the mechanism had been set to go off at one-thirty.

On the hangar floor was a large drum of lubricating oil. He dropped the bomb into it. After being saturated for a few seconds, the devilish mechanism would no longer be able to send them sky-high!

"Whew!" The young inventor whistled. "That was a close call!"

Once more Tom ascended the steps to the Flying Lab, determined to get to the bottom of this latest fiendish move by the enemy. As Tom reached the floor level of the first deck, he saw a figure staggering toward him.

"Dad, what's the matter?" Tom cried, springing forward to assist his father down the steps and into their private office.

"I—I was gassed—by that scoundrel Berg."

"Berg? He's a phoney?" Tom exclaimed.

"Yes."

When they reached the office, Tom stepped up the air conditioner and trained one of the vents directly on his father.

"That's better, son. I feel stronger already. Guess I'm lucky not to have passed out for good in that closet where Berg left me."

"How long ago did he gas you? It's one-thirty now."

"It must have been just before one, because the men weren't back from lunch."

Tom told his father about the bomb, saying it must have been Berg who had set it to explode at one-thirty. But why at that time. It would not have taken him that long to escape. The impostor must have planned to stay around a few minutes. Tom had a sudden idea.

"Dad, the office was open when we came in. Do you have your key?"

Mr. Swift felt in his pocket. "It's gone!"

"I'm sure Berg took it then," Tom said. "He hoped to find something in this office."

Rapidly he pulled out one filing-cabinet drawer after

Snatching the bomb, Tom dashed out of the Sky Queen

another. It was not long before he had the answer to Berg's intentions.

"The sketch for the Damonscope is missing!" Tom cried.

He telephoned the guard at the main entrance, asking if Berg had checked out.

"At one-twenty. And left the amulet he had on," the guard replied. "Is something wrong?"

Tom told him what had happened.

"Did Berg leave in a car?" Tom asked.

"Yes, a taxi from Riverton."

"You got the licence number, of course."

"I have it written down—it's 06–392," the guard said.

"Good! It's a clue!" Tom hung up.

As he was about to call the police, Bud knocked on the office door. Tom opened it.

"Hey, skipper, don't inventors ever starve to death?" he said. "Your mother——"

Tom interrupted and told Bud of the attack on Mr. Swift.

"Wow! Those spies are getting bolder," the co-pilot said, and asked Mr. Swift how he was feeling now.

"Stronger. But I'll feel much better when Berg's in jail."

While Tom was phoning details to Captain Rock at headquarters, Bud declared he was going after Berg himself. He asked his friend for a description of the man.

"Take a couple of plant guards with you," Mr. Swift directed. "You may run into trouble."

As Tom hung up, he realized that his mother was still waiting for him and his father to bring a guest home to lunch, so he hastened to inform her by telephone of the unusual circumstance, but assured her that his father was all right.

"I think we'd better have lunch in the office," Tom said. "Chow will fix something for us."

When Chow heard what had happened he was furious. "Brand my bones, Mr. Swift!" he cried. "I'd like to tie that attacker o' yours to the meanest bronc in Texas an' let him run all the way to South America!"

The Swifts smiled at Chow's vehemence. Then Tom asked the irate cook to prepare some lunch. While waiting, he put in a long-distance call to Señor Ricardo at his hotel in Riverton. When the scientist heard the news, he shouted:

"Of course that Mr. Berg was an impostor! Our Señor Berg does not fit that description—he does not even wear eyeglasses."

Upon learning that the impostor knew the pass-word Bapcho, the señor was even more disturbed.

"There must be a spy among the members of Hemispak!" he cried. "I'll take steps to correct this at once!"

Tom thought it was too late to do any good, but merely asked the señor if he had sent the telegram about a visitor coming from his country.

"Si, si," Señor Ricardo replied. "And our Señor Berg will visit you today. Please, to be sure of no more impostors, ask him to show you a picture in his pocket of his little boy Juan on a swing. No impostor will have that picture."

As Tom said goodbye, Chow opened the door. He was carrying a tray. Mr. Swift was not able to eat much, but his son finished every bit of the food Chow had prepared.

He was drinking a second glass of milk when the intercom phone buzzed. Tom picked it up.

An excited voice said, "We're holding a man out here at the main gate who insists upon seeing you. But something's wrong. He's given the same name as that other visitor."

"You mean José Berg?" Tom asked.

"That's right."

"I'll come over," Tom replied. "The other one was a phoney."

A few minutes later he entered the reception room of the gatehouse. Sitting in one of the comfortable easy chairs was a neatly dressed stranger holding a brief case.

"I understand there has been some confusion about a man who came here and used my name," the visitor remarked as he introduced himself as José Berg. "I'm extremely sorry such a thing should mar my arrival, and I suggest you check my credentials very thoroughly." He pulled some papers from his pocket.

Tom barely glanced at them. "You have a son, Señor Berg?" he asked.

The man looked surprised but answered readily, "*Si*. A little boy named Juan."

"Do you happen to have a picture of him with you?"

"Ah, indeed I have." From a wallet he took a snapshot of a small boy on a swing. Underneath had been written: *Juan Berg. Tiene cinco anos de edad.*

Tom smiled. "That's proof enough," he said. "Will you come with me and meet my father?"

As they went outside, Tom explained to the gateman that this visitor was really Señor Berg. He was given an amulet to wear and they proceeded to the underground hangar. After meeting Mr. Swift, Señor Berg launched into the subject of uranium and how necessary it was that the rebels of the splinter state Verano did not get their hands on it.

"It would be most embarrassing for my country—Bapcho," he said. "Our foreign commitments——"

Ten minutes later the telephone interrupted the discourse.

"Tom Swift Jr. speaking," the inventor said.

"This is Bud. Listen, Tom. We found the cab driver. He took that phoney Berg to his own plane at the Oakmont field. He had to gas up and have one of his magnetos checked before taking off, so he's just left. Maybe you can catch him. The plane's a Renshaw and it's flying south. It will probably pass right over the plant."

"I'll try to pick him up!" Tom cried, slamming down the receiver.

Turning to his father and Mr. Berg, he relayed Bud's frantic message, adding, "I'll keep in touch with you, Dad."

"Take Hank Sterling with you," Mr. Swift insisted. "You may need help."

A few minutes later Tom was piloting one of the two-seater propeller-driven planes down the runway.

"Keep a sharp eye on the sky to the east and west, Hank," Tom directed the blond, square-jawed young engineer.

They flew for several minutes in silence at full throttle. Scanning the horizon ahead of them, Hank said suddenly:

"I see something far ahead."

Tom's alert eyes shifted from his instrument panel to the sky in front of him. There was a Renshaw dead ahead, and they were rapidly gaining on it.

"Hey, that guy's swinging around!" Hank shouted.

"He's probably going to land," Tom murmured, "but I don't see any airstrip."

A minute later the Renshaw dipped behind a stand of tall pines and was lost from view. Tom whirled over the trees just in time to glimpse the plane taxi-ing into a large shed at the end of a meadow. Behind the shed stood an old farmhouse.

"A private airfield!" Tom exclaimed. "I didn't know there was one around here."

Circling over the long meadow, which served as a runway, Tom banked to land. Making a short, sharp approach, he put his flaps and wheels down, throttled back, and glided into a smooth landing.

"There's no way of concealing ourselves," he told his companion, "so be prepared for anything."

When the plane had been braked to a stop, Hank jumped out, but Tom delayed a moment. Reaching down to a small box underneath the pilot's seat he clicked on a switch and adjusted two small knobs.

"Now Dad and the folks at home will know where we are, Hank," he said.

This was a radio homing beam, a recent invention of Tom's, which would send out a constant signal until he came back and shut it off. The signal flashed at both the Enterprises plant and the Swift house.

"If your father suspects any funny business, he'll send help. Is that the idea?"

"Right."

There was no one in sight as Tom and Hank strode determinedly toward the shed into which the fugitive's plane had been rolled and the door closed. Reaching it, Hank tried to swing the door open.

"Locked," he said.

Tom pounded on the panel. "Open up in there!" he commanded. "We know you're inside!"

"That's where you're wrong!" said a cool, calculating voice from around the corner of the shed, as four heavily armed men surrounded them.

Chapter XII

OUTRAGEOUS RANSOM

RESISTANCE by Tom and Hank was futile. There was a brief struggle, then their hands were bound tightly behind them.

"Don't try any funny beesness," one of the armed men cautioned.

"Don't worry, Miguel, they won't have a chance," another answered. "We'll tie 'em up Indian style."

There was no doubt in Tom's mind that at least two of the men were Verano rebels. The other two, he decided, were North Americans. All four were tough-looking characters.

"We'll deliver these hombres to the *capitan*," Miguel ordered, after Tom and Hank had been securely bound. "He will be pleased to see them, no?"

"Where are you taking us?" Tom asked defiantly.

The answer was a shove from the other olive-skinned man, while the North Americans guffawed loudly. Tom and Hank were prodded along a path to the farmhouse. They were led through a small hall which opened into a large, well-furnished room. A young man with sleek black hair reclined in a chair smoking.

"I breeng some veesitors, *Capitan* Canova!" Miguel announced. "You are ready for them, no?"

The *capitan* was not, as Tom had expected, the fake José Berg, but the man who had slugged him at the

Enterprises plant! He was the spy who had attended the Hemispak meeting in Riverton.

"Ha! The Junior Tom Swift? So we meet again!" He gave an ugly laugh. "You expected to see someone else? My pilot friend Fernando who call himself Berg? He is gone. And you bring a friend. We will have much time to become acquainted, Mr.——"

Instead of replying, Tom flared, "What do you mean, much time?"

"Time to carry out a plan," jeered Canova. "We will talk about that later. First, I will tell you that I, Pedro Canova, am not a scientist to be crossed. You understand?"

"We admit you're cunning enough," Tom replied. "You came down a copter ladder into our grounds and shut off the radarscope."

Canova's face broke into a smile of satisfaction. "Yes, and I have other means to gain my purpose. I will keep you both for a while—as hostages!"

Miguel laughed. "The *capitan* is very smart," he said. "*Capitan* Pedro Canova and his humble servant will get big reward when we get back to——"

The leader's fist smashed down on a table top.

"Quiet!" he roared. "Would you tell these men all you know?"

Miguel lapsed into sullen silence. Pedro Canova turned to Tom.

"I have written a note to your father," he said. "You will sign your name under mine."

"Why? You want money from him for our release?"

Canova leered. "In return for you and your friend, I shall accept your Flying Lab as a present—and you will help me get it!"

"What!" Tom shouted.

Hank was too shocked by this outrageous demand to exclaim. Both listened in amazement while the rebel leader continued his demands.

"Yes, if the famous Mr. Swift wants to see his son alive again, he will leave the Flying Lab at a certain spot south of the border. Your father will then return home, and I will pick up the plane and fly it back to my country."

"You couldn't pilot it," Hank spoke up. "You'd probably pull a wrong lever and blow yourself up."

Canova frowned. "I might have to take Tom Jr. across the border to give me a few lessons!"

"What makes you think my father would agree to such a crazy proposition?" Tom cried.

Pedro Canova's evil face twisted into a warped smile as he showed Tom the note. It read:

Mr. Swift: If you want to see your son again you will prepare the Flying Lab for delivery to me. You will be informed within a few hours as to the time and place of delivery. You will keep this information in strictest confidence.

Ordep

"Ordep?" Tom repeated to himself. Then he realized what it was—Pedro spelled backward!

What should he do? He could refuse to sign of course. On the other hand, if he did sign it, his father would know that Tom was in trouble.

But how to thwart these criminals? As he pondered, Tom recalled a conversation between his father and himself only a week before, in which they had mapped out a plan in case of trouble. He would use it!

"Okay, untie my hands," Tom said. This was done.

Quietly he reached for the pen offered by Pedro Canova. Writing his name, Tom crossed the final "t" with a long, bold stroke. This meant Tom was in trouble but might be able to handle the situation himself. In any case, Mr. Swift was to stall off any proposal by the enemy as long as possible. Then Tom's hands were tied behind his back again.

"Now, you are being smart." Canova smiled triumphantly. "Co-operate with us, and you won't get hurt! By the way," he added, peering intently at Tom, "what are those coloured pencils you are carrying?"

Tom's heart leaped. His secret gadgets! Trying to sound nonchalant, he answered:

"I use various coloured pencils on my draughting board."

"I will look at them," Canova said.

Helpless to stop him, Tom watched as the man removed the green one, which contained the mini-radio. He hoped Pedro Canova's treacherous eyes would not detect the secret button which operated it. After a quick glance, Canova replaced it.

"Toys for *muchachos*," he snorted. "Play with them when I untie you!" he taunted, and did not bother to look at the other pencils.

In Spanish Canova ordered the prisoners held in his office while he went off to see about having the note delivered. Tom and Hank pretended not to understand, though both could speak Spanish fluently.

"Make sure their feet are tied," Canova commanded Miguel. "Post one guard by the door and another outside the window."

"*Si, si, Capitan.*"

Miguel inspected the ropes that bound Hank, then came over to Tom. After the swarthy villain had checked the boy's wrists and ankles, he pulled the bonds even tighter, so that they cut into the flesh. Leaving Tom and Hank lying on opposite sides of the room, he went out and slammed the door shut behind him.

"I'm glad they didn't gag us," Hank whispered. "I suppose it wouldn't do any good to shout. It certainly burns me up to think of your father being forced to give up the Flying Lab."

Tom told him of the ruse he had tried, adding, "There's a chance we can get free ourselves."

"How?"

"The red pencil in my pocket is the midget soldering iron. Back up to me, Hank, and see if you can pull it out."

The engineer inched over to where Tom lay. Though the movement made the bonds cut painfully into his wrists, he managed to twist his hands up to Tom's shirt pocket.

"I have it. Now what?"

"We'll try to sit up back to back."

This manoeuvre was painful, but they accomplished it. Hank held the tiny instrument while Tom unscrewed the cap.

"Now press the button," Tom ordered, "and hold the pencil point against the cords on my wrists."

"Okay."

The crayon end retracted, and in its place a tiny iron appeared. In a few seconds it was glowing cherry red.

As Hank was about to start burning Tom's bonds, a key turned in the door lock. With lightning speed Tom threw himself to the floor in one direction, Hank the other.

Miguel poked his head inside the room. Satisfied that his prisoners were still under control he grinned.

"American inventor caught like rat in trap!" he crowed and closed the door.

"Another one of those," Hank groaned, "and I'll be a goner."

Tom sniffed. "Burnt wood," he remarked. "The iron burned the floor."

"And my hand," Hank answered. "Well, let's get this job over with."

They resumed their back-to-back position. This time there was no interruption as Hank pressed the soldering iron against Tom's bonds. The rope began to smoulder. In a few minutes the hot metal had burned through the last fibre.

Tom's wrists were free! Quickly he untied the ropes binding Hank and those on his own ankles.

"What a relief!" Hank sighed. "I guess we'd better keep those ropes handy in case Miguel visits us again."

"Right. And I guess escape before dark is hopeless."

"Suppose they bring us some supper. We couldn't face being tied up," Hank said apprehensively.

"We'll tell 'em to leave it," Tom replied, peering carefully outdoors into the growing dusk. "But I don't think those hombres are going to think about our appetites."

"I hear men in what must be the kitchen," Hank remarked presently.

The noise grew louder. Evidently the men were celebrating, for there was loud, rough talk and laughter, partly in English, partly in Spanish.

An hour later the party ended. The murmur of voices died out altogether, and there was even a low snore from somewhere near them.

"It's now or never," Tom told Hank.

"How about the guard outside the window?" Hank asked.

"I'll use the snooperscope on him."

Taking the blue pencil from his pocket, Tom beamed a ray of infra-red light into the inky darkness. It revealed the ghostly outline of a man standing near a low fence.

"He's still there," Tom reported. "Say, he's moving. Probably going for some chow. Now's our chance!"

As quietly as they could, the two prisoners raised the window and stepped across the sill.

Running as noiselessly as possible, they stole past the shed in which Canova's plane was stored and headed for Tom's own craft.

Suddenly the stillness was broken by a droning whir just above them. A helicopter was settling down almost on top of them!

Were Pedro Canova and his pilot friend in it?

Chapter XIII

STRATOSPHERE HOP

THERE WAS little time to decide what to do. With no hiding place, Tom and Hank would be spotted the instant that portable landing lights might be turned on.

"Listen!" said Hank suddenly. "That sounds like our new four-place helicopter."

"It sure does," Tom agreed. "Maybe the pilot's coming in on the homing beam of our plane! Let's find out."

Pulling the green pencil radio from his pocket, and using a nickname Bud had given him, he said:

"Mr. Fixit to copter. Mr. Fixit to copter. Who are you? Over."

Seconds later the tiny pencil vibrated to the reply. "Copter to Fixit. This is Bud. Your father's with me. Are you down there?"

"Almost directly beneath you. Ground's clear. Hurry down!"

"I'll let the fuel out of our plane," Hank offered, "so nobody can chase us."

"Good idea," Tom said.

While he directed the helicopter to a safe landing in the darkness, Hank ran to the plane and opened the drains of the fuel tanks. Hurrying back, he reached the helicopter, which had landed, just as voices sounded in the distance and the farmhouse windows blazed with light.

"Let's get out of here pronto!" Tom urged.

He and Hank climbed aboard. As the helicopter rose into the air four powerful flashlights stabbed paths of light across the meadow. Shots whizzed below them.

"We're out of range, thank goodness!" Tom cried in relief.

"Sure, let 'em pop away," Bud agreed.

"I'm certainly glad you two are safe," Mr. Swift said. "That homing beam did the trick."

"Did you receive a letter from our kidnappers, Dad?" Tom asked.

"I did. That's when I got hold of Bud. The quicker we get the law on those gangsters the better."

Broadcasting on the police frequency, Tom quickly told his story to Captain Rock.

"Pedro Canova!" the officer cried. "He's a former convict and a renegade scientist. You were clever to outwit him, Tom. But try not to land in his clutches again!"

Captain Rock promised that state troopers would be dispatched immediately both by car and by helicopter. Thought the roads leading to the spot were bad, and landing risky, they would make every effort to get there before the kidnappers could escape.

Bud, meanwhile, guided the Swifts' helicopter over the outskirts of Shopton and soon was over the well-lighted Enterprises field.

Early next morning the telephone rang in the Swift home. The call was for Tom.

"Police headquarters. Captain Rock speaking. No luck last night," he reported.

The captain said the kidnappers had fled in their own plane by the time the troopers had arrived.

"And there's more bad news," he said. "They burned your plane."

"Burned it?"

"We found nothing but the charred remains."

"Well," Tom said ruefully, "that's better than stealing it. Thanks a lot for the good try."

Before Tom and his father left the house, Ripcord Hulse arrived in a taxi. He declared himself completely well and ready for the test hop. Over a second breakfast he gave the Swifts some amazing information.

"I've just learned," he said, "that the Air Force deserter I'm trying to find falsified his name and birthplace. He's a Eurasian by the name of Leeskol. He has joined up with a rebel state in South America called Verano."

"What!" Tom cried. "He's probably one of the gang that's been the cause of our troubles." At a nod from his father, Tom told Rip some of the details of their secret mission to outwit the rebels.

Mr. Swift mentioned that though rebels the leaders apparently had both sufficient money and education to carry out their plans. It was suspected that they were holding certain top-notch Hemispak scientists from whom they had forced vital information under threats against their families.

"A bad situation," Rip agreed. "By the way, would you have room for an extra passenger to Verano, if I can persuade Uncle Sam to send me there?"

"Indeed we would," Mr. Swift replied. "And now for your preview of the *Sky Queen*."

About a half-hour later when they reached the second level of the mammoth ship, Tom unlocked the door to the laboratory and rolled back the fireproof door. Rip stared in astonishment. Then, as they went from one laboratory section to another, he exclaimed:

"Why, this is fabulous!" he gasped. "I've never seen anything like it!"

"You sure haven't," said a voice behind him and Chow came in. Tom introduced him. "This ole lab," the cook went on, "has got more bottles than the biggest drugstore in the world. An' look at them tools!" He pointed to one wall of the laboratory. "If there's one kind missin' from that there collection—well, brand my cactus, I'll eat a pound o' Texas sand!"

Another section of the laboratory was given over to numerous machines ranging from tiny scales to an ore crusher. Many of them were unknown to Rip, who shook his head in wonder at the neat arrangement of the manually and electronically operated devices.

"Tom, kin I show Mr. Hulse the lights?" begged Chow boyishly.

"Sure. Go ahead."

Chow went from one battery of lights to another. The Swifts were amazed that he had picked up so much information from listening to the engineers when the various switches had been installed.

"This little fellow"—the cook pointed to a midget green bulb—"that don't connect to nothin', jest needs impulses out o' the air to make it light up. An' this giant here—shut your eyes, Mr. Hulse—it's fearful powerful."

The pilot did so, and Tom explained that this was really his father's giant searchlight with a few new improvements, and no one would use it unless he was wearing special lenses to protect his eyes.

"What's this gadget?" Rip asked as the tour neared an end.

"The Swift Spectrograph," Tom answered, unable to keep a note of pride from his voice. "In a matter of a split second you can analyse anything, including radio-active ore."

"Well, all I can say is, congratulations." Rip grasped Tom's hand. "I'd call this a scientist's dream come true."

Tension and excitement ran high at the Swift Enterprises as news spread that the giant craft would be given its test hop the next morning. Tom and his father met Rip Hulse and Bud at the plant early, with all the engineers and mechanics on hand.

After a last-minute check-up in the underground hangar, Tom turned a switch on a wall panel. As if by magic the roof slowly split in two. Huge gears lifted half the structure to one side, the other half in the opposite direction.

"Okay," Tom shouted to one of his engineers. "Ready for the elevator."

Slowly the hydraulic lifts pushed up the floor beneath the Sky Queen. When the edge of the floor came even with the ground level, the elevator stopped. Four rubber-tyred tractors pulled the plane out to the flying field.

"What a beauty!" Rip exclaimed. "Even better than the preview, Tom!"

Engineers and workmen exclaimed over the giant plane as it was towed to a specially marked spot on the runway. The area, a quarter of a mile square, was made of special ceramic brick to withstand the blasts of the atomic lifters.

The onlookers, standing at a safe distance to avoid being burned, cheered and shouted as Tom and the others went to their designated places. Tom took the pilot's seat, Rip the co-pilot's seat. Bud stood directly behind them.

Mr. Swift had decided to station himself in the laboratory where he could watch the reaction of the flight on the various chemicals, bottled liquids, and the electronic equipment. Everyone flipped on his intercom phones, and Bud took charge of the one to the plant, so that Tom could give his undivided attention to the test.

"Chow, are you in the galley?" Bud asked.

"Yes, Bud. But brand my maverick, I'm shakin' like a bowl o' jelly."

Before starting the ascent, Tom flipped on the audiogyrex, which he had designed to eliminate the elevator sensation in rapid rising. Then, gripping the throttle, Tom poured atomic power into the jet lifters. As the crescendo of sound increased to a frightening roar, the Flying Lab began to rise. In a matter of seconds it was shooting skyward.

"We're airborne!" Bud cried jubilantly. "Oh, brother, did we leave old Earth in a hurry!"

At two thousand feet Tom eased off on the lifters. The mammoth craft stood still in the air, as if supported by an invisible giant's hand.

"Dad, we've done it!" Tom exclaimed, gazing down at the cheering throng far beneath them.

"We have, son!" came the excited reply over the intercom. "Your invention is another great step in scientific advancement."

"What about the laboratory?" Tom asked.

"Everything took that sudden rise as well as we did. Those pressurizers are beyond expectation."

Rip slapped Tom on the shoulder. "Magnificent! This will be a great boon to the defences of our country," he commented.

Bud leaned forward. "I didn't think you could do it, Tom. This plane is just one step this side of a trip to the planets."

"Hold on! Not so fast!" Tom laughed. "Verano first."

Bud was now listening to Hank Sterling on the ground. He relayed the message.

"The crowd down there can't believe what you've done, Tom. And do you know what?" he added with a chuckle. "You've tied up automobile traffic for miles around. People are parked on all the roads, looking up at you."

Tom grinned. "We'll give 'em another show in a minute."

Assured that all parts of the plane were functioning smoothly, he applied the forward thrust. As Bud watched the air-speed indicator he gasped. In a matter of seconds, it seemed, the Flying Lab was cutting through the air at a thousand miles an hour.

"Great day!" he cried. "You could get around the world before sunset!"

"Better throttle back, Tom," Rip advised. "This is only a test."

"Right."

"And I'd advise you to take her up higher, before your enemies catch on to all this."

"Okay."

To the spectators below, the big plane suddenly looked like a meteor in reverse. The lifters accelerated the Flying Lab so fast that it was out of sight in thirty seconds.

"S-stop—stop!" Chow shouted from the galley. "Brand my dogies, I don't have enough food for a trip to Mars."

"Then we'll stop off at the moon for supplies," Bud answered.

The plane's altimeter suddenly stopped at fifty thousand feet, then began to register a drop. Tom knew after a quick glance at the instrument panel that they were in trouble.

"What's the matter?" came Mr. Swift's anxious voice from the laboratory.

"I've burned out half of the jet lifters," his son answered solemnly. "I guess the metal they're made of can't take that terrific heat."

Instantly he resumed horizontal flight.

"I'd better take her down immediately," he said. "No telling what effect it may have had on the rest of the ship."

"Yes. Don't take any unnecessary chances," Mr. Swift said, adding, "Everyone fasten his safety belt."

Rip was frowning. "Is your runway long enough to land this big ship under horizontal power?" he asked, plainly worried.

"It wasn't designed to handle anything this big," Tom replied, "but——"

He quickly gave Bud a message to relay to Hank:

"Clear the field and prepare for an emergency landing. Jet lifters conked out."

Mr. Swift came from the laboratory to watch operations. "Can you make it, Tom?"

"I hope so, Dad, but I may have to try that hairpin manoeuvre."

Everyone sat tensely while he guided the great aircraft downward in tremendous sweeps. As he turned into the traffic pattern of the Enterprises field, the airstrip looked frighteningly small. When the plane banked into the groove, Tom lowered his wheels and flaps.

He then cut off the power. The wheels touched the ground and the giant craft hurtled along the runway. Could he stop it in time to avoid a disastrous crack-up? Tom wondered.

Chapter XIV

A BRILLIANT FORMULA

"THE HAIRPIN turn! It's the only thing that will save us!" Tom murmured grimly. The runway was too short for the giant ship!

With a big stone wall looming ahead of him, he applied full left rudder and brake. At the same instant he gave the starboard engines a spurt of power.

In a flash the *Sky Queen* swung around, so that it faced the other way. It was racing at great speed toward the wall. But now when Tom opened the throttle and gave the engines full power, the terrific thrust of the jets worked as a brake to overcome the momentum of the plane. In a few seconds the ship came to a stop.

No one spoke for some time. Then finally Rip Hulse, putting an arm across Tom's shoulders, said:

"That, my friend, was the greatest piece of flying I have ever seen."

Bud leaned forward. "Pal, it was superb! I thought we were dead ducks."

Mr. Swift added his praise. "If I ever had any doubts about your invention and the way you could fly it, Tom, they're gone now."

"Thanks," said Tom simply, adding, "What about Chow? I hope he's okay."

As they left the cabin to find out, they met the cook. His face was ash white and he was trembling. Seeing the others unharmed seemed to reassure him. As they filed outdoors, he said:

"I'm sure glad to be on this here planet agin." Then his good humour returned and with a grin he added, "Even if it ain't in good ole Texas."

By this time the ground crew, led by Hank, had arrived in one of the crash trucks.

"Thank goodness, you're safe!" Hank cried. "Anybody hurt?"

Tom assured him that none of the passengers had been harmed and the undercarriage had stood up to the strain admirably.

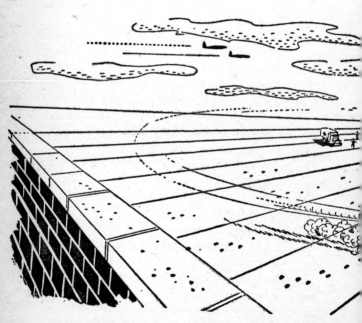

The runway was too short for the giant ship—the Flyi

"I want it thoroughly checked, though," Tom said.

He then explained that some of the lifters had burned out.

"We'll need new ones, made of a metal with greater heat resistance. Have you any ideas, Dad?"

"Not on the spur of the moment," Mr. Swift replied, but he promised to give the problem careful thought.

An hour later when Tom went to talk to him, his father said he had not solved the problem as yet, and that he had received an urgent message from Washington, D.C.

...ab raced at great speed toward the stone wall

"Officials down there seem to think my advice on some problem they have in South America will help keep the Western Hemisphere out of trouble."

Mr. Swift said he knew very little about the situation, but it definitely had to do with the country they now call Bapcho.

"I tried to tell Senator Trumper, who contacted me, that I am a scientist and not a politician, but he insists I come down for a conference, anyway."

"When are you leaving?"

"At once."

"But what about our trip to Verano?" Tom asked.

His father smiled. "I should be back here by the time you have installed new lifters in the *Sky Queen*. How about trying to invent a new heat-resistant alloy?"

Tom spent the entire next day in the metallurgical lab, making various alloys of iron with titanium, tantalum, wolfram, and other metals of high heat resistance. These he carefully annealed and then etched in mineral acids to examine the crystal structure under a microscope. But when they were tested, each one failed to be an improvement over the material used in the original lifters.

Weary and discouraged, Tom tumbled into bed late that night. But with the morning sun came an idea which so excited the young inventor that he leaped out of bed with new enthusiasm and was dressed for work within five minutes.

Tom would have dashed out the front door without breakfast if his mother had not stopped him. She kissed him good morning, saying:

"Not so fast, dear. I can tell from your eyes that you have solved your lifter problem, but you must eat before you go."

Tom put an arm around his mother and accompanied her to the dining room. Over sausage and griddle cakes he explained what he had in mind. Mrs. Swift kept nodding and smiling. Tom would never know it, but she did not understand one word of the intricate details he was telling her!

"I'm sure you have hit upon the right combination of metals," she said finally, as he arose from the table. "Goodbye, dear, and good luck."

Tom's long strides changed to an eager run as he neared the private entrance of Swift Enterprises. Few mechanics had arrived for work yet, but by the time Tom had calculated the last mathematical detail of the combination of metals, two engineers came into the metallurgical laboratory. Tom's formula excited them, and when the result proved to be a success a few hours later, all of them were elated. Tom named the new material mangalloy.

"That was a masterful idea, Tom," said Rick Bower, one of the engineers. "And it was so simple too. Why didn't I think of it?"

Stan Jones, the other engineer, chuckled. "If you could do that, Rick, you could invent a Rickety Rocket."

Tom and Rick made braying sounds in protest. Then Tom hurried off to order the new jet lifters made at once.

He summoned the foreman in charge of the machine shop, who promised to have men working around the clock to complete the lifters and install them.

"But it will take a couple of days," the foreman said.

That evening Mr. Swift telephoned his family. He was delighted to hear that Tom had conquered the sole weakness connected with the Flying Lab. He also said that what he had learned in Washington involved a complicated and serious menace to the United States as well as to all of South America.

"Senator Trumper and his committee want me to accompany them to Bapcho at once, so I'll have to change my plans about flying with you, Tom. I'll meet you down there."

"Where?"

"I don't know. I'll be in touch with you by short wave."

While waiting for the lifter work to be completed, Tom was restless. As he paced the office of the underground hangar, Bud suggested that he try to solve the mystery of the symbols on the strange missile which had come down on the airfield.

"I guess I forgot to tell you, Bud," said Tom, "that I think I have solved part of it."

"How come?" Bud asked.

"You remember there were two touching triangles in the equation?"

"Yes, but don't ask me what I think they mean. What's your idea?"

Tom said he believed that they represented two identical problems, one experienced by Earth people, the other by Martians.

"And what is it?" Bud questioned.

"It could be any number of things—climate, seasons, the effect of other planets——"

"Okay. I'll let it rest there." Bud grinned.

He left his friend. Several hours later when he met him again, Tom had to admit that he had not made any further progress on interpreting the strange symbols.

"I guess solving it will have to wait until we get back from Verano," he said.

"When do we leave?" Bud asked.

"As soon as we make a successful test hop," Tom answered.

Bud asked if Tom was going to take anyone on the trip in place of his father. Tom said he had already made arrangements with Arvid Hanson, head of the model-making division.

Two days later the *Sky Queen* was ready for its second test. After the take-off, Tom put the plane through a series of tortuous tests for over two hours. The *Sky Queen* came through with flying colours.

"Now I'm going to try for an altitude record," Tom said to Rip and Bud.

With the instrument panel indicating that the lifters were working to perfection, Tom poured more atomic power into the roaring engines. The altimeter swung up, up, up—ten, twenty, thirty, fifty, sixty thousand feet! It kept soaring higher and higher!

"Tom, we're higher than man has ever gone!" Rip cried.

"Do you think it's safe?" Bud asked apprehensively. "If we go much higher we'll be hurled off into space!"

"Don't worry," the excited pilot replied. "This is as high as we are going. Is the pressure system okay?"

Bud checked the dials on the big panel. "Tight as an eleventh-inning ball game," he replied.

"Then we'll sit up here for a while," Tom said. "I want to test the automatic stabilizer."

The *Sky Queen* hung in space while the pilots and the other passengers had sandwiches and hot drinks. Half an hour later Tom said he was going down.

"I'd advise you not to drop too fast, Tom," Rip spoke up. "You know atmospheric friction plays strange tricks."

"I know," Tom agreed.

He brought the *Sky Queen* down as easily as if he had been flying an ordinary plane no more than ten thousand feet up. When they reached ground, Hank took charge of the automatic recordings, but Tom ordered him not to make them public until after their South American flight.

That evening at the Swift home Sandy and Phyl arranged a gay *bon voyage* dinner party. Rip was there, and when the party was about to break up, he called Tom aside.

"Have you got a few minutes to come over to the Swift Construction Company field and see a new plane?" he asked.

"Sure thing," Tom replied. "Tell me about it."

Rip said that a single-seater fighter plane had just been delivered to him. He hoped there would be room aboard the Flying Lab for it, and he wanted Tom to look at it and give his opinion at once.

"The pilot brought me word that I'm to do some scouting in South America for that Air Force pilot who deserted," he said.

Reaching the field, Rip pointed out the tiny aircraft, which he said could land and take off on a runway as small as a forest clearing. It was the same size as the *Kangaroo Kub*, but was geared for close-range fighting. It fairly bristled with small armour. Nozzles of tiny cannon and midget rocket tubes protruded along the leading edge of the wings.

"Wow!" Tom cried. "That's quite a ship."

"I call it the *Bolo Fighter*," Rip rejoined. "Strictly experimental. Well, do you think you'll have room for it?"

"Sure thing," Tom answered. "Fly her over to the Enterprises field now, and we'll put her aboard in the morning."

"I'll do that."

As Rip started off, Tom went to a telephone to inform Roberts, the night watchman, that Rip was on his way over.

"By the way, Roberts," Tom asked, "have you heard anything from your son lately?"

"Not a thing. His wife is extremely worried. I hope that you find out something about him while you're in Bapcho."

"I'll certainly try," Tom promised, and hung up.

The next morning Rip's plane was rolled aboard the Flying Lab. Mrs. Swift, Sandy, Phyl Newton, and her father were on hand to wish the travellers Godspeed.

"Do be careful, Tom," his mother begged, "and don't take chances."

Tom, Bud, Rip, Chow, and Arvid Hanson climbed aboard the gleaming ship. They stood in the open doorway a moment to wave goodbye. Then the door was rolled shut.

Soon the great nuclear engines roared to life. Minutes later the *Sky Queen* was off on her maiden trip!

Chapter XV

OPERATION JUNGLE

IN LITTLE OVER an hour the *Sky Queen* was flying above the Caribbean, nearing the South American mainland. A short time later it headed inland.

"Look out, Tom!" Rip shouted as they reached a wooded area. "A plane's coming at us from two o'clock!"

As Tom manoeuvred out of the way, he caught a glimpse of a sleek European jet fighter as it flashed across the nose of the *Sky Queen*.

"That guy must be crazy," Bud howled.

"He may be crazy, but he's making deliberate passes at us!" Rip warned. "Here he comes from eleven o'clock."

"He's firing on us!" Bud cried, as a bullet went below them. "If he puts a hole in this pressurized cabin, we'll be gone gooses!"

Already Tom was getting more altitude, as Rip, grabbing binoculars, shouted:

"I believe that's the fellow I'm looking for! I'm going after him in the *Bolo*."

Quickly Rip zipped himself into a heavy insulated flying suit and rushed to the Flying Lab's hangar, followed by Bud and Hanson. As he hopped into his plane, they started the electric motors to open the rear door and then catapulted him into space.

The enemy pilot, seeing the *Bolo Fighter*, immediately went after it. He closed in on Rip with a vicious dive, forcing the ace to bank and climb in an attempt to shake the attacker off his tail. All this time a stream of tracers was ripping into the edge of the *Bolo's* wing.

With a lightning-like loop Rip Hulse suddenly whipped up and over and got on the other ship's tail. Before the enemy pilot could get out of the way, Rip fired a burst of .50-calibre bullets into the other plane's fuel tank.

"Rip hit him!" Bud cheered. "Look at the smoke!"

"The fellow's baling out," Tom cried. "There he goes and his chute is opening."

Then Rip's voice sounded clear and calm over the Flying Lab's radio. "Hulse calling the *Sky Queen*. Hulse calling the *Sky Queen*."

"Come in, Rip," Tom directed.

"This is my man, all right. I'm staying with him. Go ahead on your trip, Tom. Good luck. Out."

They watched as Rip followed the parachuting pilot down to a large clearing. Suddenly the *Bolo* began to wobble.

"Hey! Rip's in trouble!" Bud cried.

Tom lowered the *Sky Queen* for a better look. Rip would indeed have difficulty reaching the ground without a crack-up.

"I'm afraid one of his ailerons is damaged," Tom said anxiously. "I'm going after him."

As Tom prepared to land, Rip's voice came again.

"Hulse to *Sky Queen*. No need for help. I can land okay."

"Roger. But we'll stand by."

The *Sky Queen* waited, while every member of the crew, including Chow who had come to the cabin, watched the chase below.

"Well, brand my tall pines," Chow exclaimed presently, "that lil ole *Bolo* sure made a right purty landing in that forest clearing!"

Meanwhile, the disabled fugitive had crumpled to the ground, his chute almost enveloping him as it collapsed. When Rip reached him, the flier put up some resistance, but the ace quelled him with a right uppercut to the jaw. Five minutes later he spoke again to the Flying Lab over his portable belt transmitter.

"This is Leeskol, all right. He won't give any more trouble. I have a full confession, and papers I found on him prove he's working with Pedro Canova. Leeskol was hired by him to stop your trip in case you got this far, Tom. It's all part of the plot to get that uranium."

As Rip paused, Hanson muttered, "We're lucky that guy didn't knock us out of the sky."

"Leeskol figured his best bet was a surprise attack," Hulse went on. "Incidentally, I got another name from him. Watch out for a Fritz Manuel."

"I sure will," Tom replied. "What are you going to do with your man, Rip?"

"Fly him back to civilization."

"But what about your plane? We'll wait until you look it over."

After an examination, Rip changed his mind about needing assistance. Not only had the aileron been damaged, but his prisoner was becoming obstreperous.

"I'll be there pronto," Tom answered.

Just before he set the *Sky Queen* down in the clearing there was a cry from Bud.

"Look! Indians!"

A band of some dozen mahogany-skinned natives, bows and arrows poised, were moving toward Rip and Leeskol. But a moment later they were retreating among the trees, evidently frightened by the approaching *Sky Queen*.

As the plane settled on the ground and everyone

started to get out, Chow waved a stout rope he was carrying.

"I'll tie that Leeskol up myself! Nobody can double-cross Uncle Sam when I'm around an' get away with it!"

While Tom and his engineer were busy making use of the Flying Lab's equipment to repair the *Bolo's* damaged aileron, the Indians suddenly appeared again.

"They're going to shoot!" Hanson cried. "Run!"

"Wait!" Chow cried.

To everyone's amazement, he stepped forward and haltingly spoke a jargon of guttural sounds. Slowly, smiles of understanding broke out on the faces of the Indians.

"What are you telling them?" Tom asked.

"That I fetched 'em some presents from the Lone Star State."

"Presents?"

"Sure thing. I'd never get caught in Injun country without some lil ole knick-knacks."

From a pocket he pulled several cheap bracelets, rings, brooches, and four pearl necklaces, and distributed them.

"Great way to stop a fight," he commented with a grin.

It took an hour to put the *Bolo* in shape for the air, but finally Rip flew off with his prisoner.

"The Flying Lab's first relief job," Hanson remarked.

"Operation Jungle," Bud said.

Several Indians followed them back to the plane and watched curiously as the crew entered the *Sky Queen* and rose into the sky. Soon afterward, Chow brought the travellers lunch.

The group had hardly finished eating when Rip Hulse radioed them again.

"Come in, Rip," Tom replied.

"Government report says a commercial transport plane made a water landing in the Pacific. They suspect one of the passengers may be Fritz Manuel. The *Sky Queen* could get there in no time. How about it? Over."

"We'll go! Where is the plane?"

After Tom had been given the approximate position, he signed off and headed his craft for the Pacific. Half an hour later he started the search, cruising along only a thousand feet above the water. There was nothing to be seen on the calm blue-green expanse except an occasional whitecap.

"I'm afraid we're too late," Hanson muttered.

"Yes," said Bud. "They probably drowned as soon as the plane hit the water."

Tom was about to agree when his keen eyes noticed a tiny speck far to their right.

"Maybe that's a piece of the wreckage," he remarked, banking in that direction.

Bud trained a pair of binoculars on it. "Say, something on it's moving!"

"People!" cried Hanson as they flew closer. "On a life raft!"

"Bud," said Tom, "how about taking over while I rescue those folks with the *Skeeter*?"

"Sure thing."

When the twelve survivors saw the helicopter shoot from the Flying Lab, they cheered frantically. Hovering over them, Tom let down the ladder and took the men aboard three at a time. As he ferried them to the big plane, they were loud in their thanks. Tom asked their names. He was not surprised that none said Manuel, for he felt sure that the rebel would be travelling under an assumed name.

Though nervous and bedraggled by their experience, the visitors cast incredulous eyes about them as they were escorted to the lounge.

After they had been made comfortable, and Tom was certain there were no serious cases of injury or shock, he began to question them.

"I'll radio news of your safety," he said. "How many were on the plane?"

One of the survivors was a steward who said there had been twenty passengers and four crew members. At once Tom ordered a further search, but gave it up when a rescuing helicopter and a boat from shore took over. He radioed the pilot of the helicopter to be on the lookout for Fritz Manuel, and if he should be picked up, to hold him for the authorities.

"Now we'd better get back on our course," Tom told Bud.

"How about our extra passengers?"

"We'll leave them at the nearest airport." He consulted a map. "There's one due east about three hundred miles from here."

"Be there before you can wind your watch," Bud said.

"You lose. It's self-winding."

Before Tom had gone fifty miles, Bud gave a yell. "What in blazes is going on?"

A red warning light on the instrument panel was flashing on and off rapidly.

"Good night!" Bud cried. "That's the signal on the escape hatch! It must be open!"

Tom raced down the stairway three steps at a time. Arriving at the escape hatch, he was just in time to see a man, wearing a parachute, poised to leap!

Grabbing a stanchion with one hand to keep from being sucked out, Tom lunged at him.

Chapter XVI

DARING PURSUIT

THE CHUTIST dropped from the hatch before Tom could grab him. At the same instant the huge ship banked sharply. The violent turn, coupled with the suction caused by the air rushing past the open hatch, threw Tom on his face and nearly catapulted him out into space.

With every ounce of strength he held on to the stanchion with one hand and gripped the edge of the hatch with the other. There was an intercom phone only a few feet away. The electric button to close the hatch was just behind him. But both of these were out of reach.

The landscape whirled crazily below Tom, who was beginning to feel faint. Inch by inch he was being drawn through the opening. With his last bit of reserve energy he dug his toes in and forced himself back.

But it was no use. As fast as Tom pulled back, he was sucked forward again. Just as he felt himself blacking out, Tom became aware of lights and a clicking sound. The door to the hatch had closed.

"Tom!"

It was Hanson's voice. He turned the young inventor over and shook him.

"Tom!" he cried again.

In a moment Tom's senses returned. He looked at

*The man dropped from the hatch before
Tom could grab him*

Hanson gratefully, and in a weak, hoarse voice thanked him for the rescue. Presently he sat up.

"What happened?" Hanson asked. "Who opened the hatch?"

"One of our passengers," Tom replied. "He took a chute and jumped."

"Who was it?"

"I don't know."

"He must be crazy to risk his neck that way when he didn't have to," Hanson remarked.

"Maybe he had to take the chance," Tom said. "I think he's Fritz Manuel using another name, and——"

"And didn't dare take a chance of being arrested at the airport," Hanson finished.

"I'm going after him!" Tom announced suddenly, getting up.

"Over my dead body you will!" Hanson exclaimed. "If you've lost your senses, Tom Swift, I'll have to pound some into you."

Tom was persuaded to give up pursuit when he realized that his harrowing experience had left him pretty shaky.

"I'll send Bud down in the *Skeeter*," he said. "Will you go with him?"

"Yes. But do you think we can get there in time? That chutist has a good head start."

Tom picked up the intercom and spoke to Bud, giving only the briefest details and asking him if he would turn back and try to spot the chutist.

"He's not down yet," Bud reported in a few moments as he circled over the parachute.

At this announcement Tom felt a surge of returning strength. He hurried from the hangar and up to the lounge where the passengers were sitting, completely unaware of the excitement.

"One of your group has jumped from the plane," Tom announced. "Who was it?"

The startled men looked at one another, and finally a slender, elderly man said, "It was Señor Gordana."

"We think he may be wanted by the police," Tom said. "Can you tell me anything about him?"

A dark-haired man spoke up. "I was sitting in front of him in the other plane. Just before we crashed I heard him babble 'I mustn't die. Verano needs me.'"

Tom's suspicions were confirmed. Picking up the intercom, he asked Bud to get the helicopter ready immediately and go after the chutist.

"Hanson will go with you," he said. "I'll take over the controls of the *Sky Queen*."

By the time Tom reached the pilot's seat, Bud was in the hangar. The mammoth door at the rear was opened and the *Skeeter* was launched. It dropped quickly, almost over the spot where Fritz Manuel was disengaging himself from his parachute. But before the helicopter touched the ground, the chutist was racing off across a field.

"You stay here, Hanson, and guard the copter," Bud said. "I'll take care of Manuel. I'll give him a body block that'll land him back in the States."

He raced after the fleeing figure that was just disappearing into a patch of woodland. Reaching the spot, Bud listened. There was not a sound.

Too late Bud realized he was making a target of himself. The only way to outwit the fugitive was to hide and wait for him to make a move.

Dropping to the ground, Bud crawled along behind

some bushes for about fifty feet, then stood up and peered from behind a tree. He spied his quarry far ahead, running wildly along a trail.

Bud dashed after him as fast as the tangled under-growth would permit until he reached the trail. When he came to the end of the trail, he found himself near a small farmhouse.

In the distance Bud saw Fritz Manuel climb into a battered old car. With a clatter it bounced down a narrow lane and was out of sight before Bud could reach the farmhouse.

An excited woman darted out of the house. Three dark-eyed children were clinging to her skirt. Gestur-ing wildly and shouting something in rapid-fire Spanish, she called on all the supernatural powers to punish the thief who had stolen the family car. Turning suddenly she accused Bud of being in league with the thief. Speaking Spanish hesitantly, Bud explained the circum-stances. A look of fear came into her eyes.

"A foreigner!" she shouted, backing toward the house. "Where did you come from? No car, no horse——"

Still talking, she gathered her children about her and slammed the door. Bud smiled wryly despite his failure, then turned and trudged back to the helicopter. As soon as he and Hanson boarded the *Sky Queen*, Bud radioed to the airfield dispatcher that Fritz Manuel had escaped. The dispatcher promised to notify the police at once.

Tom asked Bud to take over while he went to speak to the passengers again. He wanted to tell them the plans for landing.

As Bud switched on the mike in order to receive landing directions from the airfield tower, he called to Tom, "Want me to use the elevator, Captain, or go down the spiral staircase?"

Inasmuch as there was an adequate runway, Tom thought it advisable not to reveal the fact that the Flying Lab had jet lifters.

"Staircase, Lieutenant," he answered, "and watch the bottom step!"

As the *Sky Queen* came to a stop in front of the small administration building, it was immediately surrounded by a crowd of onlookers. Tom thought they were only curious to see the huge, new-type ship, but he soon learned that several of them were newspaper reporters.

"Wheech one of you ees Mr. Tom Swift?" asked one as Tom and Bud stepped from the plane.

Tom acknowledged that he was, and at once the men demanded a story about the rescue of the group adrift in the Pacific. It was not until each survivor had been questioned that the reporters turned again to Tom and congratulated him on his magnificent ship.

Though Tom would have preferred that no pictures be taken of the *Sky Queen*, cameras were clicking busily. He tried to dodge the photographers, but this, too, proved to be impossible. Finally he called a halt.

"The planes from your country—they are so powerful," one of the reporters spoke up. "How beeg and speedy can you make them?"

Tom smiled. "Speedy enough to take all you fellows to Mars and leave you there!"

Then he excused himself and went into the building to inquire about Fritz Manuel. As he had feared, the police report was negative.

Though Tom was eager to continue his trip, he decided to lay over for a while to see if he could get in touch with his father. It seemed strange that Mr.

Swift had not sent any word to the Flying Lab as he had promised to do.

Tom put in a long-distance call to the capital of Bapcho, asking for the president's office. After a seemingly interminable wait, he was finally connected.

"This is Tom Swift Jr.," he announced himself in Spanish. "Is my father Tom Swift Snr. there?"

The reply was totally unsatisfactory. Mr. Swift, with two other men, had called on the president, but at the moment the president did not know his whereabouts.

"Perhaps you will find him at his hotel, the Plaza Lolita," the man suggested.

Tom phoned the hotel, but the desk clerk said that he did not know where the famous Mr. Swift might be found. He had not been seen for over twenty-four hours.

"Didn't my father leave a message of any kind?" Tom asked worriedly.

"No."

"Are the other men who were with him there?"

"No. They flew back to Washington this morning."

"And my father? Did he check out?"

"One moment, please." Tom could hear muffled voices, then the clerk returned. "A friend of Mr. Swift paid his bill and took his bag."

Tom's heart sank. He started to tell the clerk his suspicions concerning his father's absence, but just then the connection was broken, and Tom's efforts to have it restored met with failure.

After a moment's thought, Tom decided to call his mother. Perhaps she had heard from Mr. Swift.

"Sorry, Señor, it will take two hours to put your call through to Shopton, U.S.A.," the operator told him.

Discouraged, Tom returned to the plane. He determined to try short wave as soon as he was airborne again.

Bud was in the co-pilot's seat, listening to a local broadcast. When Tom revealed his misgivings about his father, Bud was inclined to take a cheerful attitude about the matter.

"Buck up, Tom. You know how your father is. He probably came across something in Bapcho that gave him an idea for an invention, and he went off to see about it."

Tom conceded that there might be logic in Bud's idea, but he reminded his friend that Bapcho was not too safe a place for a Swift to be. It was just possible that through a ruse the Verano rebels had captured his father.

"At this very minute, Bud, they may be torturing Dad along with John Roberts and the other scientists! We must find out!"

Bud stared at his friend. "If that's true, we'd better hit the sky road to Verano!"

The rest of the crew was summoned. After a discussion it was agreed that if the scientists were being held, they were probably in the vicinity of the suspected uranium deposits.

Tom consulted his maps, then took off, setting a straight course for the mountain which according to the Indian legend contained radio-active material. He flew high enough to avoid the soaring peaks and possible detection by their enemies.

Meanwhile, Hanson tried to contact the Swift home, then the Enterprises plant by short wave. His efforts were futile and finally he gave it up.

"Bud," Tom said an hour later, "take over, will you?

And cut down our speed. I want to try out the Damon-scope."

Going into the multi-chambered laboratory with Hanson, Tom led the way down the central corridor to an ultra-modern darkroom. The compact photographic laboratory was equipped with large and small cameras, wall-sized enlargers, a photostat machine, and a micro-film outfit.

Tom slid open a drawer and pulled out the special roll of film which he had made for the camera. After inserting it into the Damonscope, Tom hurried to the lower deck of the *Sky Queen* and fitted the lens into an aperture built just for this purpose. Five minutes later the film had been activated and automatically developed. When he removed the contents, the inventor gave a shout.

"Hanson! Look at these pictures!"

Chapter XVII

THE HOMING MISSILE

"WOW!" Tom cried. "The mountains that we just flew over must be made of pure uranium."

Hanson laughed excitedly. "It's terrific, all right."

The film from the Damonscope was entirely covered with huge black blotches. In contrast to the tiny, infrequent markings the camera had picked up before, this latest find would indicate the presence of tremendous deposits of exceptionally active ore.

"It must be practically solid down there," Tom exclaimed.

He grabbed the intercom and told Bud.

"Bank and retrace your course," he said. "I want the exact latitude and longitude of the mountain we just crossed."

Hanson acted as navigator while Tom inserted more film in the Damonscope. Five negatives were wasted before they duplicated the heavily blotched one. Then Tom called out:

"Where are we, Hanson?"

"Above the north-east corner of Verano."

"We're in rebel country," Tom said. "Now our real work begins."

Everyone was acutely aware of the dangers that lay ahead. The intercoms became silent as Bud circled the area awaiting instructions. Tom went forward and the boys discussed the possibility of landing.

"It doesn't look good," Bud remarked, gazing down at the panorama of peaks. "Not a level area anywhere."

"There's no use landing too far away from that uranium," Tom replied. "We'd never be able to trek back to it on foot over this terrain."

Bud circled again, skimming a snow-capped mountain-top.

"There's a place to land—right between the uranium deposit and that low peak!" cried Tom. "Before we go down, I want to try getting in touch with Shopton first and see if there's any news about Dad."

Tom clicked on his short-wave radio-telephone which was beamed to both his office and home. "I was thinking Dad might have met some scientist who had a solution to—— Hello. Hello, Mother! . . . Yes. This is great getting through to you. . . . We're fine. . . . Have you heard from Dad? . . . No? . . . Don't worry. I'll find him. . . . I've been busy. . . . Everyone at home okay? . . . Yes, I——"

Tom hung up as static eliminated further conversation. Turning to Bud, he told him that his concern about his dad was mounting. Although the older scientist sometimes lost track of time when he was working on a problem, one thing he never failed to do was to keep in touch with his family if he could.

"I'm sure Dad's in trouble," Tom declared. "I'm going to get in touch with Bapcho's president again and ask him to start a police search."

Unable to contact the president, he called the police chief direct. Due to the secrecy of the Hemispak project, Tom did not want to reveal all of his reasons for suspecting foul play. The chief, satisfied with Tom's explanation of not being able to locate his father, promised to start work on the case at once and offered to send a police plane out to the wild country over which Tom was flying.

"The sooner it gets here the better I'll like it," the young scientist said.

"It will be there in about one hour," the chief assured him. "Our new twin jet will be at your disposal."

"Good work, Tom," Bud said. "How about your taking the *Sky Queen* down?"

The boys had barely exchanged jobs when Bud noticed something peculiar on one of the mountainsides not far from the place where the presence of uranium deposits had been detected.

"Look!" he exclaimed.

A thin spiral of black smoke was rising from a spot located among huge rocks and boulders. At first the boys thought it might be a forest fire, but they discounted this theory because of the sparse growth near the spot.

As if to confirm their thoughts, the smoke suddenly began to act in a decidedly controlled fashion. The thin, continuous spiral disappeared completely for a moment. Then there was a short, abrupt puff.

"What's going on?" Bud asked, perplexed.

Tom did not reply but held the Flying Lab still in mid-air. There were two more short puffs, then nothing.

"If that's meant to be the Morse code, it's the letter S," Tom remarked. "Three short puffs or dots!"

"For Swift!" Bud exclaimed excitedly.

"Or S O S. Look! Here comes some more."

A long, larger puff went skyward. This time it was followed by two more of the same size and timing.

"That's an O!" Tom exclaimed.

Both boys waited tensely for another series of three short puffs that would complete the universal call for aid. But no more smoke signals came.

Instantly the same idea flashed into the minds of the two boys. Was the smoke an interrupted appeal for help from Mr. Swift, or perhaps the missing scientists they had come so far to find?

"Or," Tom wondered aloud, "is it some kind of trap?"

"If it is," said Bud, "I vote we stay up here until the police come. I have an idea your old friend Pedro Canova may be waiting for us down there. And I'm not looking forward to meeting him."

"Me either." Tom managed a grim smile. "I want to meet Canova again, but I want to do it under my conditions."

For the next hour Tom cruised slowly about the area. There were no more smoke signals and no sign of an approaching plane, though the boys kept a sharp lookout for the police.

As Tom guided the *Sky Queen* over the treacherous terrain, weather conditions changed and the pilot had moments when, because of the up- and down-draughts created by the steeply rising mountains, a second's hesitation would have been fatal.

"Some of these thermals are really terrific," he told Bud. "They would be great stuff to fly a glider over! A pilot could break an altitude record every time he got off the deck."

At the end of two hours there was still no sign of the escort from Bapcho. Arvid Hanson had joined the boys and was gazing anxiously about him.

"I certainly hope nothing has happened to those policemen," he mused. "I'm beginning to wonder if the rebels of Verano could have listened in on your call and intercepted them."

"That's an idea, Hanson," said Bud. "Maybe they were forced down."

"We'll look for them," Tom said.

He set a course straight for the capital of Bapcho but proceeded at slow-cruising speed so that all those in the plane might carefully scan the ground below.

"Not a sign of them," Tom said finally, after they had travelled two hundred air miles. "I'll radio the tower and find out if they've left."

This time he was unable to contact either the airfield or police headquarters and finally gave up.

"I'm going back," he announced.

Taking a different and longer route, the travellers still kept sharp watch through a telescopic lens for any sign not only of the missing scientists but of any camp site they might have. Nothing was visible.

"What now?" Hanson asked, as they once more neared the terrain from which the smoke signals had come.

"We'll go down in that landing area I found," Tom decided. "Okay with you fellows?"

"Sure," they answered in unison over the intercoms.

As Tom throttled back and started to descend he detected a puff of white smoke miles below them.

"Somebody's firing at us!" he told Bud. "But if it's ack-ack, they've another guess coming. They can't reach us at this altitude."

The boys scanned the sky for a shell burst. When none appeared, Tom was seized with a feeling of curiosity.

"Flip on the radar, Bud."

"Roger."

Instantly the scope above their heads revealed the ghostly figure of a moving object.

"Tom! What's that?"

"You've got me. It's not a plane. But it's coming closer."

Instinctively Tom sent the *Sky Queen* into a speedy climb.

"We're not shaking it off!" Bud yelled. "I've never seen anything like this before."

Tom grabbed his binoculars and focused them on the strange object which was rapidly overtaking them. "If it's what I think it is," he said tersely, "we're up against a demon of an enemy."

"How do you know, Tom?"

"That thing is a magnetic homing missile. If it touches us, we'll be blown to bits!"

"Look out, Tom! Here it comes!"

The young inventor kicked left rudder, cartwheeling out of the way as the missile, a flat saucerlike affair, whizzed past to starboard.

"Good grief!" Bud shouted. "It's turning and chasing us!"

Tom had read about a weapon like this in scientific journals. Perfection of such a magnetic homing bomb, which would cost a fabulous amount of money to build, still was considered several years off. Was this the first one, made by a nefarious enemy? And was the Flying Lab to be the test victim of this lethal aerial barracuda?

With only seconds to figure out his defence in a game of life-and-death tag, Tom suddenly sent the *Sky Queen* into a screeching dive.

Bud braced himself. "Tom, what are you doing? We'll crash!"

Tom had no time to reveal his strategy. The big plane shot earthward, aiming straight for a towering peak!

Chapter XVIII

CAMOUFLAGE

"THIS IS IT!" Bud whispered weakly as a crack-up on the mountain peak seemed imminent.

But Tom knew what he was about. Bringing the nose of the *Sky Queen* up in a split-second timing, he missed the mountain-top and zoomed skyward again in a manoeuvre that flattened Hanson and the boys to their seats and drained the blood from their heads.

Then came an earsplitting explosion as the bomb, carried downward with terrifying momentum, crashed into the mountain and disintegrated. Tom had out-manoeuvred the missile's homing device.

"Whew! That was too-oo close," Bud said, opening his eyes. "You can mop the floor with me, Cap. I'm a wet rag." Then, slapping Tom on the shoulder, he added, "I thought you'd gone loco. Boy, you really can handle this crate."

Tom mopped his brow. "I guess it's been only a couple of minutes since that missile shot up at us," he said, "but it certainly seemed like hours to me."

Hanson was grave. "We're not facing amateur scientists on this jaunt," he said. "They're going all out with the most up-to-date methods to stop us."

"You're right," Tom said between clenched teeth. "And we mustn't waste any time rounding them up."

"You mean you're going to Hemispak headquarters?" Hanson asked.

"No. To investigate those smoke signals. There may be more of them."

"Probably not until tomorrow," Bud remarked. "It'll be dusk in a few minutes."

"That makes it ideal for us to land," Tom said. "To avoid any more bombs and make it seem as if we've been frightened and are running away, I'll pretend to head for home."

"But you'll circle back behind one of these mountains and come in from the rear." Bud grinned.

"Exactly." Tom grinned back "If we make a low-altitude approach and landing, I may be able to set the *Sky Queen* down without any spies from Verano spotting us."

Tom flew far across the border into Bapcho territory before turning the Flying Lab around, then circled back on a much lower level. Skimming along as close to the mountainous terrain as he dared, he took the ship straight down and landed in the small valley he had detected hours before.

"You did it!" said Hanson. "I'm sure none of our enemies would suspect we'd attempt a landing."

Tom was not so optimistic, but at least the *Sky Queen* and its passengers were safe for the moment. The three got up, stretched, and went toward the door. Tom, however, insisted that they wait until he brought the pressure inside the ship to approximately that of the outdoors.

"Take it easy," he advised. "We can't rush around in this rarefied atmosphere."

"Desolate-looking country," grunted Bud, first to lower himself to the rough ground.

"Can't say I'd care to live here," agreed Hanson, following him and looking around. "I wonder how far above sea level we are."

"I think about eight thousand feet," Tom replied. "Enough to make one lightheaded."

"If you think we're up high now," Bud remarked, "take a look at that mountain next to us. From down here, it seems to be ten miles high!"

Chow, tumbling from the plane, twisted his neck up for a better look. He was speechless for several moments, then said:

"Where's the top? I jest ain't got good enough eyes to see through clouds an' snow. An' say," he drawled, shuddering a little, "the longer you look at it, the more you think it's goin' to fall right on top o' you."

After the awesomeness of their situation had worn off, the group got down to the business of settling themselves for the night. Tom, disappearing within the ship, came out a few minutes later dragging a huge sack. The others sprang forward to help him.

"Now we'll do a little disappearing job," he commented, as the burden dropped to the ground and he began pulling out a roll of netting.

"How you goin' to do that?" Chow asked.

"This net is painted with various shades of browns and greys," Tom answered, "and it——"

"Camouflage!" Hanson exclaimed.

"You guessed it," Tom nodded. "We'll spread the net over the whole ship. From the air it'll look like the ground."

"Well, brand my lil ole fish pole," Chow said with a chuckle, "I sure never saw a fish net that big. Meant for a whale, ain't it?"

"If you can find one around here," said Bud, "we'll lend you the net to catch it in."

"You jest wait!" Chow threatened. "I'll ketch somethin' yet!"

"A cold, maybe," Bud jibed.

It took the combined efforts of all four of the party to manoeuvre the tremendous nylon netting over the body and wings of the plane. For half an hour they sweated and strained, but at last the job was done.

"Now, unless someone spotted us as we came down, or had a radar bearing on us while we were in flight," Tom remarked, "it should be pretty hard to locate the Flying Lab."

"Are we going to dig tonight for that stuff what's goin' to make us all rich?" Chow asked. "I sure could use any extry wad of bills."

"That'll be Tom's next neat trick," Bud spoke up. "How to turn uranium into a bank roll in one easy lesson."

Tom grimaced, then said, "I suppose we could start digging, but it might be better just to scout around and get our bearings. It'll be totally dark soon."

After locking the *Sky Queen's* hatches as a security measure, the foursome spent an hour exploring the valley. Tom carried a Geiger counter of the standard type and it clicked steadily.

"We seem to be walking around a hotbed of radio-active substance!" Hanson commented excitedly.

"Yes," Tom replied. "And those rebels mustn't get hold of it and sell the stuff to some power outside the Americas. I'm afraid that's what they're up to."

"No doubt," Hanson agreed. "Leeskol's confession practically proved it!"

At last, puffing from their activity over the rugged terrain, the foursome returned to the Flying Lab just as darkness fell. Chow cooked a tasty, refreshing meal. Then they all sat down in the lounge to while away the hours in conversation.

Suddenly Tom held up his hand for silence.

"What's wrong?" Bud asked.

"Listen!"

There was a faint whistling sound far away, but plainly discernible through the open ports.

"A plane!" Tom cried a moment later, and led a rush for the radar screen. "Maybe it's the police."

In the cabin he quickly switched on the radar and in no time the screen showed a pip.

"Circling right over us!" Bud announced.

The group stood with eyes glued to the screen, as the tiny spot of light slowly revolved on the face of the radarscope. Was the pilot friend or foe?

"Do you suppose they know we're here?" Bud asked.

No one could answer that question. The mysterious jet craft continued to circle above them.

At last Tom broke the silence. "Let's go outside. Maybe we can see who it is."

He hurried toward the main departure hatch. Out on the cold, dank ground, with the Flying Lab blacked out above them, the group gazed skyward.

"There are the wing lights." Bud pointed toward the winking red and green lights sweeping over them.

"I'm going up!" Tom announced. "It's full moon. Come on, Bud, we'll take the *Kangaroo Kub*. It's fast enough to trail any plane. We'll soon find out if our callers are Bapcho police or Verano rebels! Hanson and Chow, help us with that portable runway, will you?"

The husky Texan and the engineer lifted one end of the netting and slid the lightweight aluminium strip down from the sliding doors in the rear of the Flying Lab's fuselage. Then they beamed lights on the ground, shielded so that the reflection would not be seen from the sky. Meanwhile, Tom had warmed up the motors of the *Kub*. Built for a quick take-off, it rolled out, zipped along, and was off the ground in a few seconds.

"I'll keep our lights off," Tom told Bud. "If possible, I don't want that other ship to know that we're around. It may pick us up by radar, of course, but we'll have to take that chance."

Jaw set grimly, Tom made a beeline for the other craft. Suddenly the latter's lights went out and the boys could hear that its speed had been stepped up.

"He's running!" Bud exclaimed. "That's not a police plane!"

The *Kub* streaked after it, whipping through the sky with every jet pushing to capacity.

"That fellow's moving fast," Bud commented. "And, Tom, do you realize what direction he's headed in?"

"I sure do. Deep into Verano territory. Bud, that pilot must have spotted us going down in the *Sky Queen*. But just to make sure he's an enemy, I'm going to contact him."

Flipping on his radio, Tom called again and again, "Police plane come in. Over." There was no response and at last Tom switched off the set.

Speedy as Tom's jet was, it still trailed the fugitive ship. Gradually the other plane became less discernible and presently disappeared altogether. Tom continued the pursuit, hoping to discover where the pilot might have landed.

Running full speed through a pass between two peaks, the *Kub* gave a sudden lurch and rose abruptly. It seemed as if the plane had been hooked to some gigantic crane and was being pulled toward the heavens with the speed of a rocket, completely out of control!

Chapter XIX

THE SECRET LANDING FIELD

"WE'VE HIT an up-draught!" Bud cried as the *Kub* bounced around violently.

Tom did not fight the controls. Instead, he waited tensely for the split second when the thermal wave off the mountain would cease.

Cutting back on his throttle to avoid having a wing torn off by the sudden gusts, Tom relaxed as he felt the craft suddenly surge under its own power toward the open sky above the snowcaps.

"Boy, I was beginning to think that——"

The words were snapped off his tongue by a sudden powerful side pull of the *Kub*. Tossed as helplessly as the silky fluff from a milkweed pod, the tiny jet plane yielded to the new force and side-slipped toward the sharp edge of the peak.

"The end!" Bud closed his eyes.

But Tom, fighting the muscle tension in his arms and legs, struggled to pull the jet back on course. When it seemed as if his efforts were useless, a hundred feet from the peak the *Kub* was caught in a new up-draught and shot straight over the mountain-top to safety.

"I've had enough for one night," Bud declared, his heart still pounding. "You ought to get a medal of pure uranium for that one, skipper. What say we go home?"

The trip back was uneventful and in the bright moonlight the boys found their headquarters easily. Hanson and Chow listened intently as Bud recounted the adventure.

"It sure ain't safe around here," the chef said. "Mebbe we oughta move out."

He left the others abruptly, going to his bunk. Hanson and Bud announced that they too were going to try to get some sleep. Tom, too excited to sleep, remained in the plane's lounge. He picked up one magazine after another but could not concentrate on any of the articles they contained until he came to one on Mars.

The Kangaroo Kub *sideslipped toward the sharp peak*

"So this writer thinks the 28 degrees below zero weather up there would make it impossible for anyone from this earth to live comfortably on the planet," Tom mused.

When he finished the thesis, Tom sat lost in thought. Those symbols on the missile—could they have something to do with weather and temperatures? Taking a pencil and a copy of the strange mathematical problem from his pocket, Tom began new calculations, using this as a basis.

"If Mars is inhabited, the people there would have a tough time visiting anywhere on the earth except the North Pole," the inventor chuckled. "Maybe they want to know——"

"Tom!" Bud's voice called from the doorway. "For Pete's sake get some sleep. It's three o'clock!"

"Okay, fellow. I'm going to turn in now."

The next morning everyone was up early. Chow prepared a breakfast of sausage and pancakes, then announced that he was ready for a digging expedition.

"But first I want to contact police headquarters," Tom replied. "They may have some word about Dad. And I'd like to know what happened to that police plane."

He and Bud went to the short-wave set and Tom clicked it on. There was a brief sputtering followed by several sharp blasts. In a few moments it became apparent that they could neither send nor receive any messages.

"What can be fouling it up so badly?" Bud asked in disgust.

"Your guess is as good as mine," Tom replied. "I'd say the Verano scientists are deliberately jamming the air waves."

Chow poked his head into the cabin. "How about it? Any news?"

Tom explained the situation and Chow urged that they forget it and commence work on the buried ore.

"All right," Tom agreed. "But you may have to go mighty deep," he added. "Better get two picks and shovels for Hanson and yourself."

"Well, brand my hoof knife!" the cook exploded. "How about you an' Bud? Do you two have some magic way o' pullin' uranium out o' the ground?"

The boys burst into laughter, then Tom said, "Bud and I are going to let you and Hanson find the whole deposit of uranium, Chow. We're taking the copter up to look for more smoke signals."

The group assembled outside to take stock of weather conditions. It was very cold and the men's breath steamed in the frosty atmosphere. But it was clear, and perfect for flying, Tom declared.

"Look!" Bud cried suddenly as an enormous greyish-black bird swooped over their heads. "Did you ever see such a wingspread? Why, it's at least twelve feet across!"

"That must be a condor," said Hanson. "The bird with a collapsible tube for a neck."

"He has more lives than a cat," Tom remarked. "A Peruvian Indian told me condors have been known to fly away after hanging in a noose for hours, and pistol bullets rarely injure them."

"I wonder where he's going," Bud said. "Uh, uh, there's his target."

Climbing up the side of the mountain was a vicuña. Without warning the voracious bird swooped down and aimed at the vicuña's eyes. As the nimble animal dodged successfully, the condor wheeled and flew away.

"But he'll be back," Hanson prophesied. "First he'll get the eyes, then the tongue——"

"Not if I can help it!" Tom exclaimed.

He ordered the *Skeeter* run quickly from its hangar and the two pilots climbed aboard. Tom switched on the elevators, and soon he and Bud were rising into the air.

"There comes that condor again!" Bud exclaimed. "My guess is he'll make short work of that vicuña!"

Tom steered left in a high-swinging arc that brought the noisy helicopter swooping down upon the blood-thirsty condor.

"What are you doing?" Bud cried. "Are you out of your mind? That bird could wreck us!"

Without answering, Tom shot his craft straight at the spot where the battle was being fought. The startled bird, having trapped the beast in a shallow rocky crevice, whirled in frightened retreat and abandoned its prey.

"Well," Tom said, "that's one meal he missed."

"Maybe you shouldn't have interfered with nature," Bud blurted out. "How's the poor bird going to get a meal?"

"I'm part of nature," Tom replied in defence. "I was just defending a valuable animal from a vulture."

"Maybe you're right," Bud conceded. "A vulture should stick to its clean-up job of animals already dead, but a condor doesn't do that."

Tom set his course for the area where they had seen the smoke signals the day before.

When they reached it, Bud remarked, "I don't see any now."

"Whoever sent the signals couldn't keep it up all day long," Tom replied. "I have an idea he waits until he hears a plane. I'll go lower and make as much racket as I can."

The blades whirred rhythmically as the helicopter lost altitude. For a moment Tom was tempted to land but the angle of the mountain-side was too steep. He flew back and forth, while they looked hopefully for a landing spot and for signs of smoke. They had just sighted a feasible place in which to come down when Bud shouted:

"I see it!"

There was no mistaking them—real smoke signals!

"Somebody must have seen us!" Tom cried jubilantly as he headed the *Skeeter* toward the column of smoke.

"They're going into code again—three short puffs for S," Bud counted eagerly. "Now three long ones—O. And there come three more short ones. It's an S O S, Tom, for sure!"

"Say, there's more—watch!" Tom cried. "It says 'H-E-L-P!'"

"It must be the Roberts expedition!" Bud exclaimed.

"We've got to free them!" Tom said determinedly. "And Dad may be with them."

"Look! More signals!" Bud shouted. "There's R again. O—and B. Now what?" The signals stopped suddenly. "Why, that's all! They just cut out altogether!"

Tom, too, was startled by the abrupt disappearance of the smoke. "ROB—could the sender have been sending 'Roberts' when someone caught him and put out the fire?" he mused.

"Or has someone been robbed? It could be either!" Bud suggested.

Meanwhile, the helicopter was descending and the boys strained their eyes for a close look at the spot from which the smoke had emanated. Bud grabbed the binoculars.

"I can't see a thing except a pile of rocks, Tom," he said. "Where could the sender be?"

Anxiously the co-pilot swept the glasses over the ground below. There was no sign of any opening in the mountain or of any life in the area.

"This sure is a mystery," he remarked. "Kind of weird."

"We can either land now," said Tom, "and take a chance on looking around, or come back when the police arrive."

"I certainly wouldn't land right now," Bud replied, after a moment's thought. "We might be walking into a trap. Those rebels could be using John Roberts and his group as bait."

"Bud! That's it exactly! We won't land now, but tonight, in the dark!"

"Are you cuckoo? How are we going to land in this mess in the dark?"

"We can do it," Tom said enthusiastically. "Bud, get our cans of fluorescent dye, will you? We'll outline that landing space with it."

"I see what you're driving at." Bud's eyes gleamed. "We'll come back tonight when the smoke senders are asleep and turn our ultra-violet searchlights on the field."

"Right. Our enemies won't be able to see the lights, but the beam will pick up the dye."

"Tonight we rescue the missing scientists—and maybe your dad!" Bud exclaimed excitedly.

Chapter XX

AN AVALANCHE

WHILE TOM manoeuvred the helicopter above the tiny emergency landing field, Bud lay prone on the deck with his arms and head extended through the partly opened hatch. He poured the contents of the cans of fluorescent dye in a narrow line around the rim of the field.

"All set!" he called to the pilot. Arising, he closed the hatch and returned to his bucket seat beside Tom. "Midnight can't come too soon for me," he said eagerly.

As Tom checked his navigation and set his course for their base, he began to wonder whether Chow and Hanson had had any luck in their digging.

At this very moment the two men were hard at work in good-sized pits which they had laboriously hewed out of the rocky table-land between the two peaks. Up to the moment they had found no radio-active ore.

Chow, some distance from his companion, stopped to mop his forehead. As his eyes roamed the landscape, they lighted upon a trickle of water not far away. Slowly the cook made his way to it, leaned over, and drank in great refreshing gulps.

"Even better'n Texas water," he told himself.

He straightened and was about to go back to his work when Hanson ran up and asked what he was doing. Chow told him.

"Well, let that be your last drink of mountain water in this place," Hanson advised, concern in his voice.

"How come?" Chow asked. "Water's water, ain't it? Tastes mighty sweet an' cool to me."

The engineer explained that the water no doubt was filled with particles of radio-active material. If taken in quantity it would attack the blood cells and cause serious damage to the drinker's health.

"And"—Hanson smiled in conclusion—"it would take those few remaining hairs off your head, Chow."

Alarmed, the cook's right hand flew up to his thinning hair.

"I remember that story Tom told us about water like that down here—it did funny things to the Injuns a long time ago. But say," he added, looking around, "there ain't no purty flowers like it said in the legend."

"The stream was in some valley," Hanson reminded him. "It was probably covered over long ago by a landslide."

Chow nodded, then, detecting the whir of the helicopter's blades, said, "Here come the boys."

As the midget ship eased to the ground, he and Hanson went to greet the fliers.

"I was beginning to wonder if you'd run into trouble," Hanson said to them.

"Trouble! We sure did," Bud grunted. And as the *Skeeter* was being snuggled back into the Flying Lab, he related their experience with the condor.

Then Tom told of their sighting the renewed smoke signals, and of being unable to discover who was sending them from among the piles of rocks below.

"But we're going back at midnight and find out," he said.

"I don't like your idea," Hanson said frankly. "If Mr. Swift or Roberts' party sent up the smoke signals, why didn't they show themselves when they saw your copter? Certainly your dad, Tom, would have recognized it."

"They're probably prisoners."

"Inside the mountain?" Chow asked disbelievingly.

Hanson went on to say that he was sure the smoke had been sent up by the rebels as a deliberate lure to capture the young inventor and as many of his party as possible.

"But I suppose there's no talking you boys out of going," Hanson concluded.

"None," they answered together.

After a meal and a much-needed rest they started digging. New spots were chosen, but Tom insisted that each remain within hailing distance of one another.

Chow headed toward what seemed to be the only sector with any density of growth, a patch a little distance below the table-land. For some time only the thud and clang of picks against earth and rock broke the afternoon stillness. Tom was startled when he heard Chow cry out:

"Hey, Tom! Come here! Help!"

Dropping his pick, Tom raced toward where the cook had been digging. He slipped and scrambled along the rocks, but finally with a sprint landed at the spot in less than a minute.

"Chow! Where are you?"

For a moment there was no sound. Then from a depression came a low groan. Tom hastened to it.

"Chow!"

"Oh-h-h, my haid!"

Quickly Tom knelt beside the cook's pudgy figure,

almost buried in the trench. Chow was moaning in pain and there was a large lump on the side of his head. It was swelling rapidly.

"What happened?" Tom asked, helping the cook out of the trench.

For several seconds Chow was unable to talk. Between moans and groans he tottered to his feet and stood there, rubbing his head.

"I don't rightly know, Tom. I was jest diggin' along an' doin' all right—you can see the place over there—when I looked up, an' brand my saddle, if I didn't see two Injuns all covered with paint standin' right there!"

"Indians!" Tom exclaimed. "Go on."

"I was so surprised I couldn't move. Then, before I knew what was goin' on, they up an' grabs me an' starts to wrestle me around. That was when I yelled."

"What'd they want anyway?" Tom asked. "Did you find out what they were after?"

"Why—me! They was tryin' to drag me away with 'em. But when I yelled, one of 'em dropped me quick into the gully. Then he said somethin' to the other an' they ran off."

"Come on. We'd better get back to the Flying Lab and put something on that head," Tom said. "Looks to me as if an ice pack might be a good idea. That's a nasty bump."

As he put an arm under Chow's shoulder and helped him along, Tom wondered if the unfriendly Indians might be part of the Verano group.

"They could be spies sent out to check on us," he mused. "But why were they painted? The Indians in these mountains only put on war paint for ceremonials. Maybe they were masquerading as Indians to mislead us."

The mystery puzzled Tom as he assisted the cook to the ship. Ten yards short of the open hatch they were startled by a distant *boo-oom!* The explosion rocked the mountain. Looking upward toward the sound, Tom saw what seemed to be the whole top of a cliff far above them breaking loose.

"What's going on?" Chow asked. The explosion had snapped him out of his daze. "What's that terrible racket?"

"I don't know," Tom replied, letting go of the jittery Texan to run back for a better view of the mountainside. "Someone must have set off dynamite above us!"

Now, as gigantic convulsions rolled through the earth, there was another sound—a deep rumbling.

"An avalanche!" Tom cried. "It's heading right down here! If we don't get away, it'll bury us and the Flying Lab! Chow, get in quick and I'll try to fly out of danger!"

Slamming the hatch shut after them, Tom leaped up the steps to the pilot's seat. With a lightning movement he flipped on the switches and poured power into the jet lifters.

The landslide was almost upon the plane. Through the netting Tom could see huge pieces of rock crashing down, knocking loose other boulders and earth. With ever-increasing speed the revolving destructive mass swept toward the Flying Lab.

Whoo-oo-oosh! The jet motors came to life and the *Sky Queen* rose above the thundering wave of debris. By seconds the destruction of the valuable plane and the death of its occupants had been averted!

The quick ascent had thrown the camouflage net off the big plane. It floated down and settled upon a pile of rock.

Now that Tom and Chow had recovered from the shock, they looked below them. To their relief they saw Hanson and Bud standing at a safe distance from the avalanche.

"Thank goodness, they're safe!" Tom murmured as he banked the plane to come about.

He waved to Hanson and Bud who gazed in open-mouthed astonishment at the sudden appearance in the air of the Flying Lab.

"They probably can't figure out how we got out of the way in time," Tom said with a chuckle.

Chow nodded. "It was right smart of me to get that bang on my haid when I did," he said. "Hadn't been for that, we'd 'a' still been diggin', an' the Flying Lab would be buried."

"Sure, Chow. And now where am I going to land the Lab?"

Before he had a chance to look for a spot, Chow cried, "Here comes more of that avalanche!"

A secondary explosion had just taken place farther along the mountain-side. The two in the plane gazed in horror as the mighty avalanche of rock fragments picked up momentum.

"Tom—Tom! It's headin' right for Bud an' Hanson! They can't escape!"

Chapter XXI

A HOSTILE WELCOME

THE AVALANCHE covered a wide area—too wide, it seemed, for Bud and Hanson to escape.

"Won't it ever stop?" Tom groaned as he lowered the Flying Lab.

"It's—it's like the end of the world," Chow muttered. "I never figured there was this many stones in any one place on earth."

Dirt and dust filled the air, preventing any clear view of the ground. When the fall of rocks had ended and the dust had cleared a bit, a feeling of hopelessness came over Tom and Chow. The spot where Bud and Hanson had been standing was completely covered with the mass of fallen rock. Freshly exposed springs trickled through the fragments. Stumps of scrubby vegetation lay in grotesque heaps over the landscape.

"Do you think mebbe the boys got away?" Chow asked hesitantly.

Tom manœuvred the Flying Lab over the scene. There was no sign of either Bud or Hanson. Chow patted his young friend's shoulder and tried to find words that would prolong the hope that by some miracle their companions had survived.

"Don't give up yet, Tom. They mighta run an' got out o' the way. Might even be that they hid under some ole boulder that didn't get moved."

"I hope you're right," Tom muttered. "But I haven't

seen a living thing move down there since the slide stopped, Chow."

"Let's land an' look around!"

It seemed impossible that Bud and Hanson could survive

Tom agreed and was about to hunt for a landing space when his eyes wandered toward the mountainside above the spot where the explosions had occurred. He could see two men running. He grabbed the binoculars and handed them to Chow.

"Look up there, quick! Are those the men who tackled you?" he asked excitedly.

Chow gazed at the fleeing figures until they disappeared, then said, "I don't think they was the Injuns."

Tom began to wonder how many enemies there were in the immediate vicinity. But his greatest concern was for Bud and Hanson, so he chose a level area just beyond the edge of the landslide to come down in. It was narrow and unprotected from hostile eyes, but the flier had no alternative.

Gently he lowered the *Sky Queen* and set her down. Jumping to the ground, he led the way toward the place where they had last seen Bud and Hanson. Slipping and sliding in the loose piles of rubble, they searched uncertainly over the sector in which their friends might be buried. At last Tom paused.

"Chow, we're not making any headway. Let's do this more systematically. Suppose we stay about ten yards apart and search in a straight line across the ground. When we get to the end of the slide, we'll turn around and come back across another strip."

"A smart idea," agreed Chow, whose head injury had been completely forgotten.

Together, they carefully climbed back and forth across the stretch of debris. They were on their fourth trip over the ruined table-land and had just began to despair of rescuing Bud and Hanson when Tom's alert eyes spotted a gleam of metal.

"Chow! Come here!" he called, rushing to the spot. "I've just found something!"

His heart pounding, Tom tore at the dirt around it until he had uncovered a shovel.

"One of ours!" he exclaimed and tugged at it until the tool came out. The wooden shaft was broken a foot above the metal. "Bud or Hanson must have been working here!"

"Then s'pose we try a lil diggin' of our own," Chow suggested.

While Tom kicked at the dirt hopefully, Chow returned to the Flying Lab and procured shovels and a couple of crowbars to help move the heavier rocks. Frantically they went to work and for half an hour fought and wrestled to clear at least a part of the debris away. But though they covered a wide area there was no sign of either of their missing friends.

Wiping the sweat from his drawn, tense face, Tom leaned on his shovel and glanced at his companion. "Maybe we're searching in the wrong place, Chow. After all, the landslide might have carried that shovel downhill and this isn't the place where the boys were working at all."

"Could be. Wanta try, say ten, fifteen yards up?"

"Yes. I can't rest until I know something definite about Bud and Hanson."

They moved up the slope and renewed their search. It took their combined efforts, using both crowbars, to dislodge several heavy rocks before they could penetrate the earth and smaller stones that were strewn about.

Almost exhausted, Tom called for time out, and they sat down, breathing heavily, against a huge boulder. Tom was casting about for another place to dig when Chow saw him freeze into a stare of disbelief.

"Tom! What now?"

Turning, he saw two crouched figures approaching from around a cliff. Tom's blood ran cold, and he heard the breath go out of Chow in a horror-stricken gasp.

The oncoming men were Indians, their faces painted in garish colours. Each one held a drawn bow with arrows levelled at Tom and Chow.

"Tom, we're done for!" Chow cried. "These are the varmints who almost got me before!"

There was nothing for Tom and Chow to do but remain where they were and raise their hands. Maybe, Tom thought, if they made no show of resistance, the

Indians would not release the arrows. As he sensed Chow's quivering frame beside him, he hissed:

"Keep still!"

"*I'm* keepin' still," Chow whispered. "It's only my body that ain't."

Even in the danger of the moment, Tom grinned at his friend.

For almost a minute there was no move on the part of the Indians. Never had Tom seen two bigger men than these who stood rigid as statues.

"They must be waiting for someone else," Tom thought.

At last one of the Indians relaxed a little. Watching Tom and Chow out of his keen black eyes, he eased up on his bow and lowered the arrow. With a guttural murmur to his companion, he stepped around the prisoners, apparently inspecting them for knives, guns, or other weapons.

Still under the threat of the second savage's drawn arrow, Tom and Chow did not dare make a counter-move. The other Indian circled them, finally stopping in front of the two. Now his companion lowered his weapon and moved forward.

Tom quickly decided to offer a gesture of peace. Slowly he moved his hands forward, palms out-thrust.

"Friend!" he said.

The Indians merely stared at him, their faces impassive. Almost disdainfully they exchanged several grunted words. Then, carrying their bows with the arrows still strung and ready, they moved behind their captives. Tom and Chow felt the sharp tips of arrows against their backs.

"They want us to start walking," Tom murmured to the cook. "And I guess we have no choice."

"They sure mean business," said Chow. "An' a Injun arrow ain't nothin' to monkey with."

As they walked along, the Indians stayed so close behind them that any lagging produced an immediate jab with the point of an arrow. The direction Tom and Chow were to take was decided by a momentary pressure on one side of them or the other.

Across the slope of the mountain they moved. Chow tried a question or two in dialects he hoped the Indians might understand, but the only answer he received was a sharper jab than usual from the man behind him.

After a long walk they came to a slightly wooded area where four burros were tethered among the trees. While one Indian stood off with levelled bow and arrow, the other made Tom and Chow understand they were to climb upon two of the beasts.

As soon as they were mounted, the savage tied their hands behind them. They would not be able even to use the rope halters on the burros' heads!

"This is great," Chow growled. "I'm balanced up here like a ole Humpty Dumpty. What happens if this here beast stumbles?"

"Burros don't stumble, Chow," Tom told him. "Unless you fall off yourself, that beast will carry you safely."

By this time their captors had mounted, too, still holding their weapons in readiness. Grasping the lead ropes of the Americans' burros, the Indians led the way among the scrubby trees and across a large clearing. They had almost reached the opposite edge when there was a tremendous roar behind them.

"What's that?" Chow cried. "Another landslide?"

Tom's face went ashen. "It's the Flying Lab!" he cried. "They've got that, too!"

Chapter XXII

AN EMERGENCY INVENTION

"THOSE REBELS have outsmarted us!" Chow moaned.

To his surprise and Tom's their Indian captors acted as if they did not know anything about this part of the plan. For the first time they stopped and looked about uncertainly.

"They're still keeping those doggone arrows ready, though," remarked Chow as he watched the savages, hoping for a chance to escape.

After a moment the Indians kicked their heels into the sides of their mounts, trying to hurry them along over the terrain. Their beasts did move somewhat faster, but the captives' mounts dragged.

Suddenly the roar of the jet lifters grew louder, and presently the *Sky Queen* was directly overhead.

"There she goes!" Tom cried, almost in despair as he saw his wonderful ship disappearing right before his eyes.

The very bottom seemed to have dropped out of the world, so far as Tom Swift was concerned. His father, Bud, and Hanson were gone, and he and Chow were prisoners!

Suddenly the huge plane, banking, came back and stood directly overhead. Then slowly it began to descend. The burros, completely upset by the roar, kicked and shied. Tom and Chow were sprawled on the ground.

"That fool pilot! What's he tryin' to do, crash here?" Chow yelled.

"He's going to buzz us!" Tom shouted, trying to pick himself up but finding it difficult with his hands tied behind him.

The Indians were shouting too now, uttering strange cries and trying vainly to keep their shrilly hee-hawing burros under control in the turmoil. But with the Flying Lab whizzing down at them, they gave up. Abandoning all the burros, the Indians ran for their lives. The animals, freed, took off in a mad scramble across the slope.

Suddenly the *Sky Queen* braked in mid-air as the pilot exerted control on the jet lifters. For a second the big ship hung motionless, then eased to the ground.

"They're going to capture us!" Tom muttered to his companion, who was too shaken by his fall to run.

Then a voice cried out, "Hold on!"

Turning, they saw Arvid Hanson jump to the ground. And from the pilot's window a familiar face grinned at them.

"Bud!" Tom cried.

The co-pilot joined Hanson. Together, they rushed over to their friends and slashed the ropes that bound their wrists.

"You're alive, thank goodness!" Tom cried. "But how? What? The landslide?"

Bud gave his friend a tight smile. "It missed us, Tom. Say, let's get out of here. Tell you about it in the plane."

Tom and Chow followed the others inside. The hatch

F

slammed shut and Bud threw power into the lifters. When the Flying Lab was high in the sky, away from danger, stories were exchanged.

"We just missed being buried under that second slide," Hanson related. "Bud and I ran for cover and met in a cave. We watched you up in the ship—say, how did you happen to get away?"

Briefly, Tom told of the attack on Chow and their fortunate move toward the plane for medical aid just before the slide started.

"To get to where you landed, Tom," Bud took up the story, "we had to do a lot of climbing. When we saw those two savages capture you, we were too far away to help, so we went for the ship and—well, you know the rest. We really scared those Indians when we buzzed them."

"I reckon I ought to thank you," Chow commented. "But you sure frightened me an' that burro. I thought that plane was goin' to land right on my back!"

"It's broad enough for a landing field, at that," Bud said jokingly. Then in a serious tone of voice he asked: "Where do we go from here?"

"We don't want to get too far away," Hanson replied. "But we don't want to stay so close that our enemies down there know where we are."

"Let's scout around a bit," Tom proposed.

As they cruised over the general area, Tom went on an inspection trip of the *Sky Queen* to see if anything had been damaged by the sudden ascents. Reaching the place where the Damonscope was installed, he stopped short at the strange sight before his eyes. The microfilm had been dislodged from the camera—which turned on automatically during a flight—and was lying in a tangled mass on the deck.

"It's completely black!" Tom murmured excitedly, picking up some of the film to be sure it had been developed. "Not a thing on it but a picture of radioactive ore! That landslide must have opened up a gigantic deposit!"

The inventor was so elated he ran back to report his findings to the others. Bud gave a cheering shout and added with a grin:

"Those dynamiters did us a really big favour."

"And themselves too," Tom commented. "We mustn't let them take command."

He was eager to set down at once and get samples of the ore, but Hanson laid a restraining hand on his friend.

"Some folks don't know when to give up," he said, "and you're one of them. You had a strenuous day, Tom. Why not leave the ore until tomorrow and get a little shut-eye before you start on your rescue mission?"

"You're right," Tom conceded. "Dad and the others come first."

As they reached their chosen landing spot, Bud became wary of setting down the mammoth ship in the narrow space. He asked Tom if he would prefer taking over the controls.

"I think you can do it, Bud," Tom replied. "Just be careful of the walls of that gorge. It'll be a tight squeeze."

They all held their breath while Bud skillfully manœuvred the *Sky Queen* down into the narrow cleft and deposited the plane smoothly and effortlessly at the bottom.

"That was right purty flyin'," Chow said as they stepped out onto the flat floor of the canyon.

"It sure was," Tom agreed. "Now if I hadn't lost that camouflage cover, we'd really be hidden." He squinted up at the narrow opening to the sky.

"Yes," Hanson agreed meditatively. "But even without it, a rebel plane would still have to fly exactly overhead to spot us."

Chow, remembering the landslide and what had caused it, glanced at the high rocky walls and shivered. "One lil ole charge o' dynamite up there an' we'd be buried so deep they wouldn't find us till the next century. I jest don't feel comfortable down here in this hole, all unpertected. Why don't we paint the *Sky Queen* fancy colours like these rocks? Then our enemies won't see us."

The other three stared at him.

"You've got something there!" Tom cried. "We have all kinds of paint in the storeroom."

Chow went to get several cans of reddish brown, green, grey, and purple paint, very much like the natural colours of the canyon walls and floor. All four of the party went to work with a will, each using a separate colour. Tom and Bud slapped huge strokes on the upper side of the wings, while the others painted the cabin and fuselage. When they finished, the inventor surveyed the work from his high perch.

"No one can see this plane now unless he climbs down here and looks at it," he remarked.

Chow had disappeared before the job was finished, and as Tom made his remark, the cook summoned the others to supper. During the meal, the young inventor was quiet. Bud, knowing that his friend's reticence meant that he was coping with a problem, asked:

"What's hatching, Cap?"

Tom smiled. "I'm trying to invent an imaginary aerial so we can get through to Shopton or the Bapcho capital. It's worth the chance of being detected," Tom added grimly.

"I don't see how you can do it, Tom," Hanson said quietly.

"There's one possibility," the young inventor continued. "Do all of you see those stars at the far end of the canyon, where it opens toward the Pacific? I'm going to beam a message out there and trust that some ship will pick it up."

"Sounds okay," Bud said. "But you don't have enough power to keep it from being jammed."

"Maybe we do," Tom replied.

After supper Tom went right to work. He hooked in one of the *Sky Queen's* jet engines to energize a jerry-rigged directional-beam transmitter.

"I hope, with this extra power," he explained to the others, "to beam my message straight up and over the Andes. Some operator somewhere should pick it up and relay it to Shopton."

"Won't the rebels jam this message, too?" Bud asked.

"There'll be enough juice to get it through, I think," Tom replied.

Within an hour he had perfected the experiment and was sending with his strong, improvised outfit.

"This is as crazy as using a steam locomotive to heat a hotel," Bud said, grinning.

When Tom finished transmitting, he flipped on the receiver. Only garbled sounds poured out. Chow, to hide his disappointment, announced he was going to the galley.

"That's a hopeless mess!" Bud exclaimed as the static continued.

"Perhaps," Tom replied, "but I have an idea. It seems to me that there's a chance we could decipher something out of the blur we're getting. It's worth trying."

The inventor started a tape recorder and picked up the garbled sounds for about three minutes. He then played it back, over and over again. The result was an unintelligible jargon interspersed with staccato noises like those of a trip hammer.

"No go," said Bud.

"Unless," Tom murmured, "I can erase the interference overtones and leave just the voice I want to hear."

"It's over my head."

"Suppose you had a piece of paper with a message written on it," said Tom, "and someone scribbled all over the sheet so you couldn't read the words. If you wanted to see the message badly enough, you'd erase all the scribbling."

While talking, Tom had taken the tape to his differential harmonic analyser and turned on the light. He was now studying the many series of angular graphs which showed up.

"The one with the middle-range vibrations," he said, pointing, "is a man's voice."

Carefully the inventor lacquered over the other graphs. As soon as it dried, he ran the tape through the transcribing machine. The sound of one voice came clear and distinct. Tom grinned at Bud, who grabbed up the intercom to the kitchen and shouted to Chow:

"We got through! The commander of the *U.S.S. Garner* picked up our message and is rebeaming it to a weather ship off the coast here."

"Well, brand my navy beans," the cook cried, "Tom's done it again!"

"Now all we can do is wait for an answer," Tom sighed. He glanced at his watch. "We'd better hit the blue, Bud, if we're going to solve the mystery of the smoke signals. Hanson, will you take over here?"

"I won't leave the set," the engineer promised.

Tom and Bud donned warm clothes, and Chow insisted upon stuffing the pockets of their flying suits with sandwiches. He filled two Thermos bottles with steaming cocoa and carried them to the helicopter. As Bud thanked him, he said with a grin:

"This will hold us for a while if we're captured, Chow."

The cook's eyes bulged. "Hey, just a minute! You sure gave me a different idee. Those blasted rebels are s'posed to be caught nappin'. Ain't that it?"

"Stop worrying." Tom smiled. "You're right, Chow. Bud and I are going to find out if Dad and Roberts are prisoners somewhere near where we saw those smoke signals. If so, we'll free them and bring them here."

Chow was pacified. "Okay. Good luck!"

He and the two fliers swung open the rear doors of the *Sky Queen's* hangar and wheeled the helicopter down the portable runway. In a few minutes Tom and Bud were off on Operation Smoke Signal.

Chapter XXIII

PRISONERS

THE MIDGET helicopter soared up through the canyon. Tom had to use extreme care in the darkness not to smash a blade against the walls, but with the ease of long practice and experience he soon had the craft clear of the gorge.

After pausing in mid-air to get his bearings from the various mountain peaks, he set his course toward the spot where he hoped to make the rescue. After cruising for ten minutes, he turned to Bud and said:

"I think this is the place. How about turning on the lights so we can pick out that landing area?"

Bud switched on the ultra-violet searchlights and both boys strained their eyes for the rectangular patch they had outlined the morning before. Nothing showed up.

"That's funny," Tom muttered.

He cruised over the mountainous region for several minutes without seeing any sign of the fluorescent dye.

"Hope that stuff wasn't a dud," Bud remarked worriedly.

"No, I'm sure it couldn't be," Tom replied. "Look! There it is!"

Almost directly beneath them a narrow strip of purplish light gleamed steadily.

"Now we get to work," Bud said. "I wonder what we'll find."

Tom, serious and equally curious, cut the forward
thrust of the *Skeeter*, and the little ship descended
slowly into the centre of the field. There was only the
faintest indication of a jar as the craft landed. The
searchlights were turned off, the ignition locked, and
the boys, with Tom carrying a coil of strong rope,
scrambled out.

"Got your flashlight, Bud?" Tom whispered, as they
moved cautiously away from the helicopter.

"Yes. But we'd better not use lights unless we have
to."

"Right."

"Which way shall we head?" Bud asked.

"The smoke signals came from over on our left. Let's
try that direction."

With Tom in the lead, they advanced cautiously.
Once Bud kicked a loose stone, which clattered in the
stillness as it rolled a short distance. For minutes afterward, the boys stood still, waiting for some sign that
they had been heard. When no one appeared, however, Bud said in a low voice:

"No harm done. Let's go!"

Tiptoeing along and feeling their way with each foot
before putting any weight on it, they inched their way
among the rocks.

"Hss-s-st, Bud!" Tom's hand, reaching back, tightened
convulsively on his friend's shoulder. "Look!"

To their right around a ledge of rock, were two spots
of brightness, close together. The next moment they
seemed to shrink to pin points. They went out for a
second, then reappeared.

"Eyes!" he hissed to Bud. "An animal!"

He clicked on his flashlight. Beaming it directly
ahead, he picked up the snarling face of a South

American mountain lion. The beast lowered its head, growled deep in its throat, turned, and slunk away from the light.

"Wow!" Bud murmured. "Nice, friendly little cat! Hope we don't run into any more of those! What now?"

"Keep moving," Tom instructed. As he snapped off the flashlight, he said, "I see a light way off there!"

A tiny flicker of illumination was visible in the distance. Carefully the boys walked toward it, until they could see the embers of a small campfire glowing just ahead among the rocks and stumps of the uneven ground.

"An iron gate! Just beyond the fire. It's set right into the rock wall of the cliff!"

"And there's the sentry—curled up against the rocks there by the fire!"

"He's sound asleep!"

Stealthily the boys crept forward until they were almost on top of the native watchman. On one arm was strapped an unusual wrist watch which they both recognized as the property of Mr. Swift!

"Cover the guard's mouth with your hand before he can yell," Tom directed Bud. "I'll grab his arms."

As one they leaped from their hiding place and landed on the inert form. Before the man could utter a sound or make any protest, he was completely over-powered. With rope and a handkerchief from Tom's pocket, the two bound and gagged him. He thrashed about, his black eyes gleaming balefully.

"Here are some keys," murmured Bud as he went through the man's pockets. "And a whistle. No gun."

"One of these keys should fit the lock in this gate," Tom said. "Let's try them."

Before the guard could utter a sound he was overpowered

They tried first one and then another of the keys. After what seemed an eternity, one clicked in the lock, and they were able to swing the huge gate open.

Tom considered the situation. He wondered if there were more guards inside.

"One of us ought to stay here and watch while the other goes inside," he decided. "All right with you, Bud, if I investigate?"

The co-pilot nodded and took his post.

"If anyone comes, blow the whistle," Tom whispered, and went through the gateway.

Tom snapped on his flashlight, peering through the gloom for a hasty impression of the layout. There was nothing in the cave, but far inside he could see the outline of a door.

Cautiously he moved toward this new barrier. The cave proved to be longer than he had thought. But as he walked, the ceiling and floor began to converge. Finally Tom had to crouch almost double as he neared the door. Finding it locked, he again tried the watchman's keys. The first three would not fit into the lock, but the fourth opened it with a grating sound.

"Who's there?" a voice called, as Tom extinguished his light and pushed the door open.

The man spoke English without the trace of an accent. Deciding to take a chance, Tom replied:

"A friend from the United States."

"Then come in," the other invited.

Tom turned on his flashlight and swung its beam around. Lying on blankets on the cold earthen floor, and now arising eagerly to greet the visitor, were four men. Tom knew one of them.

"John Roberts!" he cried, rushing over to him.

"Tom Swift! Where—how?"

Roberts jumped to his feet and wrung his friend's hand. Then he introduced the others, all South American scientists.

"How did you get past the guard?" Roberts asked.

"Bud Barclay and I took care of him. Bud's waiting outside. John, have you seen my father?"

"Your father? No," Roberts replied. "Isn't he with you?"

"I haven't been able to contact him for some time. I'm afraid he's a prisoner. The guard outside was wearing his watch."

"The rebels haven't mentioned him," Roberts said, "so the guard probably found the watch or stole it."

"Then maybe Dad isn't their prisoner and is all right!" Tom said hopefully. "By the way, when do you expect your jailers back?"

"Not before morning and perhaps not then," Roberts answered. "Often a couple of days go by and we see no one except the guard. It gets dreadfully cold here, so he sometimes brings us a small pile of wood to make a fire. He also brings our food, which is only a little corn-meal mush."

For the first time Tom realized how weak and haggard the men were. They would not be able to walk very far. From his jacket pockets he took the sandwiches Chow had given him and also some food pellets which he always carried for emergencies. He was sorry that he had not brought the Thermos bottles too. While the men ate, he told them that Bud and he had come because of S O S smoke signals and asked if the men were responsible for them.

"Yes," Roberts replied. "We saved the wood to burn. It was our only hope. We've been sending signals from a tiny crevice in the cave for two weeks off and on. Thank goodness you saw them."

"You've been prisoners here for two weeks?" Tom asked, looking at the dank interior of their prison.

"Yes. Our captors moved us around from one place to another, at first, and then brought us here. This is actually a century-old prison."

"Who were they? Do you know their names?"

"Oh, yes. One is Pedro Canova——"

"Canova, eh? I had a bad time with him myself."

"And another's named Fritz Manuel."

"Manuel! We caught him once—under another name—but he got away." Then Tom questioned, "Who is their leader? Apparently they're only stooges for a higher-up—someone of a different nationality, perhaps."

Roberts could not answer that question. He had only heard Fritz Manuel and Canova talk vaguely of the "boss," without learning who he was. Never had they used an actual name.

"I do know one thing, though," Roberts said. "This gang has a member who also belongs to Hemispak. I've heard Canova talk about how they learned of your plans through the information the traitorous member supplied."

Tom realized now that this mysterious person was probably the one who had intercepted the Bapcho police and engineered the attempts to harm Tom's party and ruin his Flying Lab. He wondered who it possibly could be. Each member had to prove his skill as a scientist before being admitted to the group. Who was the traitor?

"What were Canova and Manuel planning to do with you and the others, John?"

"They were going to make us work out some tests with uranium—but not until they had disposed of you and your party. You came into the picture rather unexpectedly and upset their well-laid plans."

Tom nodded, more eager than ever to outwit his enemies. As soon as the men had finished eating, he asked if they felt strong enough to leave. They assented, anxious to gain their freedom.

With Tom flashing the light, they started off. Halfway to the main gate Tom heard a shrill whistle.

As quickly as he could run in the confines of the passageway, Tom hurried toward the gate. When he arrived, his worst fears were realized. There was a chain and padlock linked round the gate—a padlock for which Tom instinctively knew he did not have a key!

Outside, in the dim light of the fire, there was no sign of either the trussed-up guard or of Bud!

Chapter XXIV

CHOW'S DILEMMA

"F-L CALLING! Ten-fourteen calling! Come in!"

Hanson sat before the short-wave set with Chow lounging near by.

"How many times kin you say that an' not lose your voice?" the cook asked. "It's jest about five hundred now."

The engineer gave him a wan smile. "When you're fighting an enemy as dangerous as the rebels, Chow, you don't give up," he said. "How about you trying it for a while?"

They changed places and the Texan began the monotonous job of trying to raise some radio ham far away. Since nothing had seemed to come of Tom's endeavour, Hanson had decided to try the old-fashioned method.

"Let's see," said Chow. "F-L is for Flying Lab. Ten-fourteen's our ship's number. How about my trying S-Q for *Sky Queen*? And mebbe TOM-S?"

"No, not TOM-S. That's too obvious," Hanson objected.

"Those boys have been gone a powerful long time. I sure hope they ain't in trouble," Chow said.

Hanson also was beginning to worry. If the boys should fail to return and he could make no contact with the outside, what should he do? Investigate the source of the smoke signals, or take a chance on flying the big plane to the nearest city for help?

"F-L cook calling," the chef said, by way of changing the routine. "Chow on the line. Over."

Despite his worries Hanson smiled. But a moment later the smile changed to a look of utter disbelief. Chow had just switched to the incoming beam when a voice said clearly and distinctly:

"Rip Hulse calling Chow. Got your boss's message."

"Well, brand my ole flyin' suit!" the cook yelled, so thunderstruck he failed to flick the switch. Hanson jumped forward to do it.

"Rip Hulse, come in," he said. "Chow and friends on F-L. Where are you?"

"Com Cincpac 1280," was the quick reply.

Chow looked blank but Hanson, a former Navy man, explained that this phrase indicated the ace flier was in the Pacific not many miles west of Lima.

"Come in! Come here! Help!" Chow shouted excited. "The Inj——"

Hanson held up a warning finger. It would be fool-hardy to give their position away to the enemy.

"Rip knows we were coming to Verano," the engineer whispered.

"S O S!" he cried into the speaker.

"Meet you in the morning," Rip promised. "By——"

Static interference cut off the conversation. Chow and Hanson wondered if it were weather conditions or the rebels jamming their wave length.

"Anyway, we got through," Chow gloated. "When Tom Swift comes awalkin' in here——"

"Tom Swift will not walk in here," said an icy voice behind the men.

They wheeled to face a dark-complexioned stranger with high cheekbones. He had piercing eyes and a sneering smile. Behind him stood several Indians. At a wave of his hand all but one retreated outside. Hanson and Chow knew they were prisoners but put up a bold front.

"Wh-who are you? What do you want? How'd you get here?" Chow burst out.

"Never mind who I am." There was faintest trace of an Oriental accent in the man's speech. He laughed softly. "I might not have seen your plane, but my Indian friends—they are good watchmen and they know all the trails in this canyon. Just behave, and you will remain alive."

"What did you mean that Tom Swift won't return?" Hanson asked him.

"The great young man—I have just heard by short wave—is my prisoner. And his famous father—he is in our hands too."

"Where's Bud Barclay?"

"I do not know. My friends—they took him away." A cunning gleam came into the tormentor's eyes. "He will make a very good pilot for us, is that not so?"

"Why, you——!"

Chow sprang forward to throttle the stranger, but he suddenly whistled and several of the Indians appeared. The cook halted.

"You see you are my prisoners also," the evil-faced man cried. "But I am a person of patience. You will have a chance to be free on one condition."

"What's that?" Chow asked.

The stranger deliberately took his time before answering. He lighted a cigarette and paced up and down for a few moments. Finally he said:

"First, I will tell you a little about myself. I am a Eurasian by birth."

Eurasian! Hanson and Chow instantly thought of

Leeskol, the Eurasian whom Rip Hulse had captured. Had the two been in league?

The man continued, "By choice I serve Europe or Asia, whichever suits my purpose best."

"You mean you ain' got a country you stick to?" Chow burst out.

"Is that so very necessary?" the man asked suavely, a sardonic smile playing over his face.

"It sure is!" Chow cried. "Why, you low-down——"

Hanson grabbed the furious cook's arm. "Better let this fellow do the talking," he advised wisely.

The man nodded. He seemed unruffled by Chow's patriotic outburst. After going to one of his companions and whispering something, he returned and faced his two captives.

Hanson kept his eyes on the Indians. The engineer had decided that if the natives left the plane he would take a chance on jumping the Eurasian and gaining control of the situation.

"To continue," the stranger said, "it suits my purpose now to take the ore from these mountains to a certain power across the Atlantic. These rebels in Verano—they are stupid. I use them but not for long. I will need more engineers—and a good cook."

"Don't look at me!" Chow cried out. "I ain't joinin' up with a bunch o' blasted rebels or Eurasian double-crossers!"

The Eurasian blinked and for the first time appeared to be angry. But he paid no attention to the cook's accusations. Instead, he said:

"You two look like smart fellows. Why do you bother with these Swifts, these Yankees?"

"What do you mean—they're our friends!" Hanson exclaimed.

"That is true, but only while they can get something out of you. Join my forces and you will be rich."

Suddenly Hanson had an idea. Escape for him and Chow could be brought about only by keeping this man and his escorts at the Flying Lab until Rip Hulse and the police arrived. The engineer decided to try a delaying action—playing along with him. Before he could speak, Chow cried out:

"What's the good o' bein' rich if you ain't got friends? No, sir, I'd never go back on the Swifts or the U.S. or lil ole Texas. Not for all the *yoo*-ranium in the world!"

"Then you will take the consequences," the visitor said.

"Mr.—er——" Hanson spoke up. He paused, hoping their captor would reveal his identity, but after a long silence on his part, the engineer continued, "There might be something in what you say. But if we're to talk man to man about it, I really should know how to address you."

At Hanson's words Chow blinked in utter astonishment, and the Eurasian looked at the engineer with a piercing stare. The American smiled disarmingly, and the other relaxed.

"I said you were smart," he remarked. "Now you are becoming sensible too. You will call me Vladimir."

Hanson coughed to conceal the elation he felt because his scheme was already working successfully.

"Mr. Vladimir," he said, "what assurance can you give me that I will become rich overnight if I join forces with you?"

"I did not promise overnight results," the man replied quickly. "There is much work to be done, but the results—they will be most satisfactory."

"But in the meantime I must have money to support my family," Hanson said.

"There is plenty of money for a very good salary for you," Vladimir said. "When we have accomplished our mission, the profits will be divided. Your share should be a large one, if you work——"

"When I undertake a job," Hanson said stiffly, as if the other had offended him, "I give every ounce of my strength and every minute of my time to it."

"I am glad to hear that," the Eurasian remarked.

Chow could stand the situation no longer. Rushing over to Hanson, he shook him until his neck cracked.

"Have you gone plumb loco?" he cried unbelievingly.

"Stand back and don't interfere!" Vladimir ordered.

Chow let go, but began muttering threats at the engineer. Hanson wanted to wink at the loyal cook to let him know what was going on, but did not dare, for fear of giving away to Vladimir the role he was playing. Completely overcome by the turn of events, Chow dropped into a chair.

"Brand my mule an' saddle!" he said and closed his eyes.

The Eurasian suggested that he and Hanson go to some quiet spot in the plane where they might talk undisturbed. This unexpected suggestion was not to the engineer's liking. Vladimir might have been pretending to believe that Hanson would join the rebels. When they were alone, the ruthless scoundrel might try to force the engineer to reveal certain secret equipment in the Flying Lab or even kill him! Hanson tried a counterproposal.

"Vladimir, is this proposition so secret that even your own men shouldn't hear it?" he asked. "We needn't worry about Chow any longer. He's in our hands and can't do any damage." Going a little closer to the Eurasian, the young man whispered, "I might even convince Chow that he ought to come over to your side."

This later statement seemed to convince the Eurasian. With a look of disdain at the figure slumped in the chair, he said:

"Let us get down to business. First, we will discuss how we can use your fine laboratory for our work."

Hanson had glanced at his wrist watch. It was nearly four o'clock. Dawn was breaking. Help was due to arrive during the morning. He hoped it would be early. If he could only keep Vladimir occupied until Rip Hulse came!

"I *must* do it!" the engineer told himself with finality.

Chapter XXV

AN AMAZING DISCOVERY

"WE CAN'T BREAK DOWN this heavy iron gate," Roberts said to Tom, as they leaned against the barrier to their mountain prison.

"Even if we could, it wouldn't do us much good," the young inventor replied. "Here comes another guard. One move on our part and he'd summon an army of Verano rebels."

As darkness turned to dawn, a feeling of utter helplessness overcame Roberts and his fellow scientists, but Tom already was beginning to figure on how he could effect an escape. Leaving the others he went back to the room in which they had been imprisoned. Perhaps there was some way to enlarge the tiny opening through which the smoke signals had been sent.

After an investigation Tom was convinced that this was impossible. The rock was like flint and there was not a tool in the place.

"Our only hope is more smoke signals that will be seen by some friendly pilot who understands them," Tom decided.

He hunted for some wood but could find none. The scientists had used up their meagre supply.

"There must be some solution!" Tom mused. Suddenly he snapped his fingers. "The rocks themselves. There must be carboniferous layers here somewhere and maybe some lichens."

Excitedly he started a search, beaming his light close to the walls. Various ores showed up, including a tiny vein of uranium. But now that seemed unimportant. And lichens he found which could be used for kindling would do no good without fuel to keep a fire going.

Tom had completely circled the cave, not missing an inch of it, ceiling, floor, and sides, and was about to return to the corridor when something caught his eye. A smile of satisfaction spread over his face.

"Perfect!" he cried.

A thin black streak ran at an upward angle from the floor to the ceiling. Tom whipped out his sturdy penknife and began to scrape. The black substance was almost pure graphite!

The knife worked quickly and efficiently. Handful by handful Tom carried the precious dust to the small crevice ready for use at a moment's notice. When he had accumulated a good-sized pile, he laid an extra pack of matches he carried on top of the flammable pile of graphite dust and hurried back to his companions. He found them still huddled beside the gate. The campfire outside had long since died to ashes, and the mountain air was chilly. Tom told the men what he had done.

"If we hear a plane, let's send up an SOS," he proposed.

"But what good will that do with the rebels in control?" Roberts asked hopelessly.

"It might be a rescue party hunting for us and bringing the police."

Another half-hour dragged by. Then hoofbeats could be heard in the distance and presently Pedro Canova came clattering up on a horse and reined in right before the gate. His black eyes looked more evil than before.

"So! We meet again, eh?" the rebel sneered

Peering through the bars, the rebel spotted Tom immediately.

"So! We meet again, eh? The so-smart Junior Tom Swift is not so smart, after all. You thought you had escape for good when you climb through that window long ago! Well, it is a smart man who does not finally get caught in Pedro Canova's net, no?"

Tom did not reply, but his silence did not discourage Canova, who continued:

"If our fire had found its mark on that plane you and your troublesome sister were in—bah! We have wasted much time since, due to your meddling!"

Tom gritted his teeth in anger.

"And you were going to keep us from the uranium!" the rebel went on. "It will interest you to know, young Señor Swift, that even now we are in complete control of the situation."

He looked past Tom at John Roberts and the other scientists.

"And since we have found the ore, we will have no need of men who will not do as we say. You become one of us or die!" he shouted, shaking his fist.

The prisoners could only stare at him in amazement. Calming down, Canova went on:

"And what ore! The richest deposit in the world— and all for Verano and her ally. It will make her the richest nation in this part of the globe. And wealth means power!"

He looked at the scientists who had worked with Roberts.

"Power, do you hear? We will control your so-called mother country, and now we shall be the stern parent, we of Verano!"

Tom had stopped listening to the man's boastings. His keen ears had caught another sound—the whir of a helicopter's blades!

"It's now or never!" he decided. "If only that pilot is friendly!"

While Canova continued to rant and rave, Tom spoke to Roberts. Fortunately, the rebel was so busy with his promises of the great things in store for Verano that he failed to notice their whispering.

"John, send up some smoke signals. Another SOS!"

"Right!"

Stealthily Roberts inched his way to the back of the narrow passage to the room where the scientists had been imprisoned, while Tom once more occupied Canova's attention.

"Where is my father?" he demanded.

"Your father, your friend Bud Barclay, and those other two—all of them Verano prisoners!" he exulted. "Every one of them. Never fear, you will see them again soon. They will be brought to this cave."

The import in the words struck Tom with immense relief. At least his father was still alive!

More questions from the young inventor started another flow of bragging on Canova's part. The rebel's eyes gleamed as he related the great plans he had for himself and for Verano.

"Just keep talking, Pedro," Tom murmured hopefully to himself. "The longer the better!"

Suddenly the man's steady stream of self-praise was cut short by the sound of concentrated rifle fire. Canova suddenly disappeared.

There were more shots, and several cries of terror. Those inside the cave could hear orders being barked in an authoritative voice.

Around the corner of the ledge just outside the gate a small company of Bapcho soldiers appeared. Two of them were dragging Canova, handcuffed, to the gate. Behind them was Rip Hulse!

"Rip!"

"Tom!"

One of the officers gave Canova a shove toward the gate. "Open it, you traitor!" he commanded in Spanish.

Cowed and beaten, Canova obeyed, and the barrier swung wide. Tom, John Roberts, and the other scientists welcomed their rescuers with joyous shouts and fervent handshakes.

"Rip! How did you happen to be here?" Tom asked when the excitement died down a bit.

"I picked up a relayed message from the *U.S.S. Garner* and got hold of these soldiers pronto," the flier replied. He introduced Captain Diaz, then said, "We've been flying around for an hour. I wasn't sure where to look for you until that smoke signal appeared."

Canova was forced to reveal where Bud was being held; then, after picking up the unharmed co-pilot, Tom said they must all fly to the *Sky Queen* as soon as possible. He was sure there was trouble there, also. The two helicopters would proceed together.

As the group walked toward their craft they saw another helicopter arriving. From it climbed a detail of soldiers whose captain announced that they had come to comb Verano and track down all the other rebels. Fritz Manuel, Miguel, and the ace pilot of the gang, Fernando, had already been captured.

Tom's flight and that of Diaz to the area where the *Sky Queen* stood in the canyon were quickly made. The captain insisted that the armed contingent go first and in a short time all the Indians and the astonished Vladimir were captured.

Hanson and Chow were unharmed. As the engineer expressed his relief and explained how he had kept Vladimir there by pretending to join his rebel group, the cook looked on shamefaced. Finally he said:

"Well, brand my ole cowhide skull, I never caught on." Then he grinned. "I'm sure glad we all got free an' are going to git home agin."

He had just finished speaking when they became aware of a small plane circling the area.

"I'm going up to the top of the canyon in the *Skeeter* and see who that is," Tom announced.

He had barely risen into the air in the helicopter when the wings of the plane dipped in recognition and two familiar faces pulled close to him.

"Dad! Señor Ricardo!" Tom shouted joyously.

As quickly as possible the two craft landed and father and son embraced.

"You escaped from those rebels!" Tom cried.

"I didn't exactly escape, son. I was released this morning from the dingy vacant house where I'd been held by Señor Bonomo. He checked out of my hotel for me and kept me closely guarded."

"Who's he?"

"The traitor in Hemispak," Ricardo replied. "The one who let Pedro Canova into the meeting. He has been working with Vladimir Contes, the boss of the gang, and was responsible for every—what you call—leak in our plans."

"He caused the jamming of the air waves and kept the police from coming here by pretending you had countermanded the order, Tom," Mr. Swift added.

"Has Bonomo been captured?" his son asked.

"Yes," Ricardo answered, "thanks to you, Tom Swift, and your friend Rip Hulse. The message you sent started the police working. The rebel state has collapsed."

Diaz's soldiers took their prisoners away, and with sighs of relief the others sat down to talk over the fortunate turn of events and let their families know they were safe. Presently Tom picked up a signal on the radio receiver. It was from FBI headquarters in Washington reporting that all the members of the rebel gang in the United States had been rounded up. Among them were the cruel couple who had tied up Sandy in the woods.

"That saves me the trouble of looking for those two," Bud spoke up. "I've lost my chance to give that guy a thrashing."

"Never mind." Tom laughed. "I can use your muscles right here. We have some digging to do."

He then proposed that they fly over to the ore deposit and obtain some of it to analyse.

"A good idea, Tom," Mr. Swift agreed.

"But not till after you eat," Chow insisted.

An hour later the whole group started off. Tom carefully eased the Flying Lab out of its tight berth and shortly afterward set it down just beyond the disastrous landslide.

Digging operations got under way immediately. It was hard work, but this time there was none of the fear that had prevailed during their earlier digging efforts. Tom was busy high on the mountainside when suddenly he gave a shout.

"Here's something! It's in this rock formation that the explosion must have pushed up."

There was a concerted charge from all sides at the cry. Mr. Swift and Señor Ricardo, with John Roberts assisting, examined Tom's find.

"This is it, all right, I'm sure," he declared, and there were murmurs of assent from his father and the other scientists.

"But what is it, exactly?" Bud asked.

Mr. Swift studied it carefully. "I don't believe it's pure uranium," he stated. "But whether it is more valuable or less, I can't say."

"Dad," Tom said excitedly, "now we can prove the worth of the Flying Lab! We'll take this ore inside and analyse it under the mass spectrograph."

Without delay a sample of the ore was taken to the

laboratory. Everyone stood by tense with expectation as Tom made the test. In a matter of minutes, he completed the analysis.

"This is one of the transuranium elements which has never been discovered!" he announced.

Mr. Swift, amazed, added, "Some of the simpler uranium elements, such as plutonium and americium, have been manufactured by man in atomic piles. This strange ore, however, seems to be a higher element. All I can say is that its atomic number is higher than any known now."

"Lucky thing our discovery didn't get into the hands of that subversive group!" John Roberts declared. "This element can be of great help to mankind, but those rebels probably would have blown us all to bits with it."

Señor Ricardo raised a hand for silence. "It is only proper that I take a moment to extend boundless thanks to the Swift expedition for the magnificent work they have done on this trip," he declared. "Tom Swift, the heartfelt appreciation of our mother country goes out to you. And to you Señor Swift, and your friends.

"And so it would be only fitting," the president of Hemispak continued with a smile, "that we give this almost-magical substance a very special name. We shall call it Swiftonium!"

"Yippee!" shouted Chow from the doorway, and the Swifts' other admirers enthusiastically took up the cry.

The next day the *Sky Queen* started her homeward journey. Bud was in the pilot's seat, Tom and his father near him.

"Well, what's the next job for the Swift Expeditionary Forces?" Bud asked.

Little did he realize that it would not be long before he would play an important part in another adventure, *Tom Swift and His Jetmarine,* followed by *Tom Swift and His Rocket Ship.*

Tom grinned at Bud and said, "Ever think of trying to get through the earth?"

"No. Too hot for me down there."

Tom looked at his father. "Have you figured out those symbols on the meteor?" he asked.

"I believe I have. Did you?"

"I think so. A group of scientists on Mars can't determine how to penetrate the Earth's atmosphere."

"That's my theory, too."

"And they want us to meet them in space to help solve the problem so that they can visit us," Tom continued.

"That's the way I interpret it."

"Well, what are we waiting for?" Bud cried.

With a laugh he turned full power into the jet lifters and the *Sky Queen* shot upward.

"Hey, hold on!" Chow objected. "I got to make a stop first in good ole Texas!"

"You'll have time while Tom's building a rocket ship," Hanson remarked. "And by the way, Tom, what about the atomic sub you're building that's going deeper in the ocean than anyone has ever been?"

Tom grinned. "Bud, you'd better head for home. I'll give those Martians a rain check."

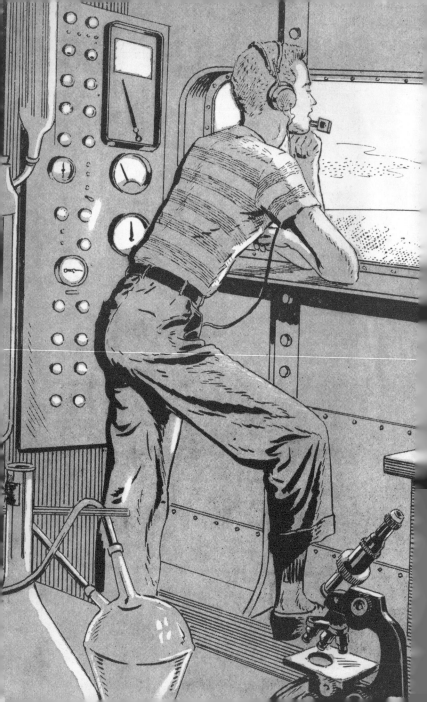